The Endra Scripts

Endra: Anecdotes of a Modern Day Witch
Phases 1 - 10

by

Polonious

The Endra Scripts
Endra: Anecdotes of a Modern Day Witch

Table of Contents
Phases 1 – 10

Endra: Anecdotes of a Modern Day Witch

Phase 1: Seeing Tarot

by Polonious

ENDRA: ANECDOTES OF A MODERN DAY WITCH

Phase 1 – Seeing Tarot

CAST OF CHARACTERS (in order of appearance):

ENDRA.........................*Energy maven living in Windover.*
KNIGHT ....*Endra's companion and lover*
MAN ON STREET.......*Angry man, spills coffee on Endra*
ALYSIA.......................*Works in Endra's office building,
                                      fashion designer*
GLENN........................*Endra's client, match to Josephine*
WORKER.....................*Random construction worker*
JOSEPHINE ....*Endra's client*
ALLISON ....*Endra's client*
CHUCK ....*Endra's client*
AL   ....*Endra's client*
HENRY........................*Owner of Henry's Flower Shop*
KATHERINE...............*Endra's client*
MAN WITH
CELLPHONE ....*Random man outside restaurant*

EXTRAS......................*Random workers at the construction
                                      site below Endra's window, various
                                      patrons and servers at Chez Jacques.*

SETTINGS IN WINDOVER:

♦*Endra's Herb Garden*   ♦*Endra's Office*
♦*Endra's Cottage*   ♦*Henry's Flower Shop*
♦*Main Street, Windover*
♦*Chez Jacques Restaurant*

Phase 1: Seeing Tarot

ACT 1

ENDRA IN HER HERB GARDEN

Endra enjoys a daily stroll through her herb garden, collecting herbs for tea.

ENDRA: Ahh, the sage is coming in beautifully. But so much? . . . Sage clears the energy. (ENDRA PUTS HER HAND ON HER CHIN AND CONTEMPLATES) Hmm, chaos must be coming my way. (SMELLS THE SAGE AND THEN SMELLS LAVENDER) First sage and now so much lavender. Sage will clear the chaos and lavender will bring comfort and love in. The energy always reveals the truth. This should be an interesting day.

Endra collects a few more herbs and walks further, bumping into branches on the ground.

ENDRA: Oh, these will make great wands to project energy.

She picks up the light branches and carries them in one arm and with her free hand she reaches up in a gesture of thanks to the apple tree. Feeling something, she grasps the air.

ENDRA: What is this I sense in my hand? This air feels hot with static electricity.

She looks around and takes a deep breath, slightly coughing.

ENDRA: (SNIFFING AND TWITCHING HER NOSE) And where is that smoke I smell coming from?

3

Endra looks up, cocks her head to the side, and out of the corner of her eye notices the sky ablaze.

ENDRA: Hmm, it looks as if bolts of lightning are burning in the sky. Oh dear, that is more than a storm.

As if agreeing, two seagulls squawk alarmingly overhead and shoot off in the direction of the darkening sky.

ENDRA: Scavengers in pursuit, chaos is there and headed this way. Indeed, sudden changes must be coming. (SHUDDERS) Maybe it's time I head into the house.

Endra carries her herbs and apple tree branches, and walks briskly towards her cottage.

Endra is sensitive to energy. Others who think they dabble in realms not of this world may mistakenly call Endra a witch, psychic, or medium. But she is so very much more. She receives messages from nature, the elements and all the energy moving around, through and within her, whether from the past, present or future.

***

ACT 2

ENDRA'S COTTAGE

Endra opens the back door to her cottage, and goes in.

ENDRA: It is so nice to be here. As opposed to out there.

Endra goes to the kitchen, picks up a teacup and places it on the table.

ENDRA: I am really looking forward to my tea today. With all the potent forces out there, my Grandmother's cup and the tea from these herbs will be most helpful.

Looking up, Endra draws her hand across the geometrically stocked herbs, spices, and kettles.

ENDRA: Hmm. Is there anything else I could make in preparation for today?

The water boils taking her attention away from the other herbs. She pours the hot water into her Grandmother's cup.

ENDRA: Well, I suppose the energy from these leaves is what's most important for me to have today. The sage is enough to clear and the lavender enough to calm.

Endra picks up the hot tea and comfortingly sips and inhales.

ENDRA: Hmm. I get the scent of rosemary and cardamom? But that's not in my tea. Ohhh, Knight. (ENDRA SMILES) Knight will love a special blend tonight. Ahh I already feel his arms around me.

Instantaneously, Endra fast forwards to the evening when she feels Knight around her. She gasps with pleasure. In the distance, a Grandfather clock chimes twice, bringing her back to the present moment, in the kitchen.

ENDRA: Two chimes from Grandfather's clock. Is there a significance to two o'clock or something related to two? The energy of time is fun to play with. I'm sure I'll find out one way or another.

Endra sits at the kitchen table, her energy returns to the evening ahead. Drinking more tea, she closes her eyes.

ENDRA: It's funny how your hands are twice mine, Knight. Has the day passed so soon?

Endra hears the sound of clinking glasses and is brought back to the present moment.

ENDRA: (STARTLED) Oh dear, what is that? Hmm, clinking glasses . . . an earthquake?

Endra walks around her cottage. She stops and listens trying to figure out what has happened.

ENDRA: I can sense something has happened. An earthquake? I didn't feel any tremors.

Endra's gaze falls upon the Grandfather clock.

ENDRA: Time will tell me all I need to know. But for now I must head to town.

***

ACT 3

ENDRA WALKING
ON MAIN STREET, WINDOVER

Windover is a quaint town with small shops lining the streets. Endra eagerly heads down Main Street.

ENDRA: Huh, isn't that odd? All of a sudden I smell sage again.

A passing car backfires loudly, as if an explosion. Endra jumps.

ENDRA: What the . . . ?

A man approaching from the other direction emits a high-pitched scream and trips, falling into Endra, spilling his coffee.

MAN ON STREET: (SHOUTS) What the hell are you doing? Didn't you see me? I'm trying to walk here. You caused me to spill all my coffee. And I just paid for it. SERENITY NOW!

ENDRA: Sir, how dare you talk to me like that! (BLOTTING HER HANDKERCHIEF ON HER CHEST) You spilled coffee all over me!

MAN ON STREET: I did?! You're an ass! Don't you even watch where you're walking?

ENDRA: (FURIOUSLY) An ass? Where I am walking? You tripped in my direction, you donkey!

MAN ON STREET: (SNARLING) Shit! (POINTING AND TIPPING OVER HIS EMPTY CUP) It's your fault there's nothing left to my coffee!

ENDRA: That's because I am wearing it!

MAN ON STREET: (POINTING TOWARDS HER) So next time lady why don't you watch where you are going! I don't have time for this crap. I'm late for a meeting and now I have to run and get another coffee!

ENDRA: (COCKS HER HEAD) Hmm. Run . . . run?

With a strong intention she shakes her hand in his direction and circles her wrist in the air.

ENDRA: I'll show you the runs, indeed!

The man rushes down the street towards the Captain Coffee shop. Endra turns and walks towards her office building.

***

ACT 4

THE LOBBY TO ENDRA'S OFFICE BUILDING

The door to Endra's building flies open. Endra enters the building.

ALYSIA: Eeeenndraaa! Eeeenndraaa!

Alysia walks toward Endra, dragging an overfilled rack of colorful blouses and skirts behind her. Alysia herself is wearing a tape measure around her neck as if it were a necklace, while a swatch of fabric is pinned to her skirt.

ALYSIA: Endra! Endra! (STOPS SHORT) Oh no! What happened to your blouse? Well that's not fashionable.

Alysia reaches into the middle of her rack sifting through blouses.

ENDRA: This menace of a man spilled his coffee on me, but nothing to worry about dear.

ALYSIA: (FROM BETWEEN CLOTHES) Oh, that's terrible. (THEN REACHES HER HAND OUT HOLDING A BLOUSE) You must take this one! It's from my latest collection. You'll absolutely love the fresh silk tones.

ENDRA: Yes! Such an intricate shade of purple. Thank you so much. So Alysia, you were calling me?

ALYSIA: (WHISPERS) I was wondering did you feel it? Did you know?

ENDRA: Did I feel or know what, my dear?

ALYSIA: This morning, it happened far north of here, an earthquake. Terrible damage. My friend Mallory called to tell me.

ENDRA: (TO HERSELF) So it was an earthquake. The clinking glasses I heard. Shattered glass everywhere, and so much chaos and damage. (TO ALYSIA) Yes Alysia, I sensed the chaos this morning. But it will calm down and your friend Mallory will be okay.

ALYSIA: Thank you Endra. You are so kind and thoughtful. Mallory said it wasn't that bad and they are all fine. (SQUEEZING ENDRA'S ARM AND WHISPERING) But funny you sensed it. Since it was so far away, the news didn't cover it. I only know about it because Mallory called me. Interesting how you knew though. I don't know how you do it!

Waving, Alysia happily turns and rolls her designs down the hall. Endra turns in the opposite direction and heads to her office.

ENDRA: (SMILING TO HERSELF) How I do it? That's funny. Energy is the only teacher I have ever known. I'm fortunate to realize that we (EXTENDING HER HANDS) all work, play and create with energy. Whether or not one is aware of this fact, doesn't change this truth. Energy is a part of everyone and everything. That is all there is.

*** *

ACT 5

ENDRA'S OFFICE

SCENE 1: GLENN

Endra enters her office, and takes a deep breath as she walks to her desk.

ENDRA: Ahh, clove and patchouli. And jasmine as well. A lot of male and female energy. Lots of love in the air. (LOOKS IN HER APPOINTMENT BOOK) Lots of love indeed! My calendar is filled with people looking for love today.

As Endra lights two candles, she intuitively turns towards her door.

ENDRA: Right on time, Glenn, come in.

Glenn enters.

GLENN: Hey Endra, so let me tell you. I'm easy. It should be simple. I have a good home, I live in a good school district, and I have a great job. I just want someone to have my kids. That's all.

Endra walks over to her marjoram and repots it from a smaller pot to a larger pot. She collects dead leaves from her other herbs, gathers the trash in her office, and readjusts pictures on her wall. In the background Glenn is talking on and on, continuing to babble.

GLENN: Hey, are you sure you're getting what I'm saying?

ENDRA: My dear boy, you might think that I'm not paying attention, yet I am listening to the vibration of every word you use. I am getting to the core of what you want and need. I am not a multitasker.

GLENN: Oh, okay, whatever works for you. I'm getting older. All the guys in my fraternity are married with kids. That's all I want. I went to a good school, I've got all the latest technology, and I just bought a new SUV. It's parked right down there. (POINTS TO HER WINDOW) Check it out. It's the black one. Pretty slick, isn't it?

Endra glances out her open window, seeing many black SUV's. Her attention is drawn to the construction site below where two men are loudly arguing.

WORKER: What the hell man?! You've been in here seven or eight times. You're a mess and you don't even work here.

MAN ON STREET: Dude, I don't know what's going on? My stomach. I haven't been able to get to my office yet! (HOLDING A CUP OF COFFEE, AS HE RUNS OFF TOWARDS THE PORTABLE TOILET)

Endra recognizes the man from the morning who spilled coffee on her.

ENDRA: Yes, the runs indeed. How absolutely divine!

GLENN: (UNAWARE OF ENDRA'S ATTENTION) My SUV is divine, isn't it? I'm also one of the youngest to make partner. That ought to count for something. And I was a star hockey player back in my day at University. I earned a lot of those trophies and plaques they have in their cases. Did I tell you I went to Harvard? Business School, that's right. It's a hard one to get into and I'm still in touch with all of my classmates. I know a lot of people. All my classmates, all my friends are married, and they have kids. That's all I want. Look, I was married before, but it just didn't work. Now I want to be married again and just have the kid part. I've got everything else.

ENDRA: (DUSTING BOOKS AND MOVING THEM BACK ONTO HER SHELVES) You do?

GLENN: Yes, I just need someone to fill the part of wife and give me kids. Just like everyone else has. I already tailgate with my buddies during football season, I have more than enough friends, and I know which private schools I'd send my kids to and what teams they could play on, already. So can you help me find kids . . . I mean, can you help me find a wife to have kids with?

ENDRA: Why do you need to have kids?

GLENN: I don't fit in unless I have them. All my friends have them. I have everything they have, and now I want kids. It's time. I mean, I'm already 41. I've got everything else. It's time for kids.

ENDRA: So you are just looking for someone who is fertile?

GLENN: Well, that's an odd way of putting it. I mean, all my friends have a wife and kids. There's nothing wrong with me wanting what all my friends have too. Cheerful, happy kids.

ENDRA: Cheerful, happy kids.

Endra sees a vision of Glenn as a little boy, with his hands under his chin, on the right page of an open book on her shelf. He is lying on the grass smiling as if daydreaming. His friends are playing near him, just as a young girl holding a kite enters the scene from a few feet away.

ENDRA: (TO HERSELF, DEEP IN THIS VISION) Isn't that girl with the kite Josephine? (ENDRA ALOUD) Interesting . . .

GLENN: Why is that so interesting? I have everything I want and am doing everything I want to do. I just want to have kids. Maybe you are just not taking me seriously. How could you know what I need? You didn't even take any notes?

ENDRA: (LAUGHS) Here's the only note you need. As you'll see on this paper, her name is Josephine, and that's her number. Call her.

GLENN: Josephine. Really? Just like that? You're sure she's what I need?

ENDRA: Quite sure. (SITS DOWN) Have a good day Glenn.

Glenn leaves. Endra lights sage incense.

ENDRA: (SPEAKING OUT LOUD TO THE ENERGY) Oh Josephine is a perfect fit. She is looking for a prince to save her from the doldrums of everyday life. She's desperate to be a mother and have kids and have someone else take care of her and provide all of life's pleasures and necessities. Yes! A perfect fit!

Later that night in Endra's office, it is dark and the telephone answering machine beeps and plays.

GLENN: Endra, it was a great night. Josephine is a princess. I couldn't be happier.

A second beep sounds from the answering machine.

JOSEPHINE: He has such a great job, and he wants so many kids, and to get me nice clothes. And he talks about vacation places we can buy. And he went to such a good school. What a great match! Thanks Endra!

SCENE 2: ALLISON

There is a quiet rapping on Endra's door.

ENDRA: (STANDING) Come in!

ALLISON: (POKING HER HEAD INTO ENDRA'S DOORWAY) Is now okay? I'm Allison. I might be a little early, but I'm eager to talk to you. Even my friends can't wait to hear what you have to say.

Endra waves her hand to enter.

ALLISON: It's not that I tell my friends everything or listen to what they say, it's just that I have a lot of good friends who love me and they want me to be happy. My friend Chuck says they swarm me. He's a goofball. My friends are just like my family. I mean, my family is great too. My sisters and brothers are always there for me. Their husbands and wives are too. They're all married. Not me though, not yet. Most of my friends are married. The one's that aren't at least have a boyfriend. Geez, I don't even have a boyfriend. Obviously you know that, that's why I'm here.

ENDRA: Certainly, dear.

Endra gathers coriander, gardenia, ginger, jasmine and lavender and simmers them in a small pot, using an apple wand to mix them.

ALLISON: Am I rambling on? I am, aren't I? I know. Chuck says I always blab when I get nervous. He always teases me when I'm nervous. I don't know why I'm nervous. I mean, all my friends and family are behind me on this. I love them and they love me back. They want me to be happy. And they know all I want is to be in a relationship. That's a funny way of putting it. I mean everyone around me is in a relationship.

ENDRA: Who is this Chuck? A suitor? (ADDS ROSE WATER AND ALMOND OIL TO THE HERBS)

ALLISON: (LAUGHS) Oh, no. He's just Chuck. Gee, we've known each other for like forever. Well maybe not forever. It has to be 20 years or maybe more. Anyway, he's a nice guy, always helping me out if I need help. But he's not my boyfriend. Oh no. I don't have a boyfriend, so, that's why I'm here.

ENDRA: Oh, that's why you're here. (STIRRING THE CONCOCTION)

ALLISON: I'm looking for someone. You know, at the last family reunion it just looked like everyone was with someone. Everyone, except me. And then, we all paired up and went on this challenge. We had to hike up a mountain. I had no one to invite so I brought Chuck. He knows all my family. Anyway, he was my 'plus one' up the mountain. We actually ended up winning first place in the challenge! I love Chuck. He always makes me laugh and surprises me, but we are just friends. Hey! If things go well with me, maybe I can send Chuck to you after.

Endra smiles never looking away from Allison, and continues throwing a few magnolia flowers into the simmering pot.

ALLISON: (LOOKING OVER HER SHOULDER) Oh, that smells amazing. You know, I am just looking for love. Someone to love me and someone I can love. Someone to get married to, who makes me laugh, who I can do things with and talk to and go on hikes with. He would have to be someone who gets along with all my friends and family. I'm looking for that love that everyone around me has. I'm tired of not having that. I want the long walks on the beach and to grow old with, you know, my soulmate. Chuck and I joke that if we both don't find anyone by the time we are 60, we will marry each other. Isn't that funny?

ENDRA: Is it?

Endra notices the brew bubbling.

ALLISON: Yes. (LOOKING BACK OVER HER SHOULDER) That really does smell amazing. Is that a special perfume or something? I'd love to get a few dabs.

ENDRA: Of course, dear. I know the perfect person for you. Just show up at 8 PM at Chez Jacques, downtown. You know where that is, yes? (ENDRA FILLS A SMALL VIAL WITH THE POTION AND HANDS IT TO ALLISON.) And dress magnificently. I will take care of everything else.

Allison opens the vial and places a few drops behind her ears, and on her neck and wrists.

ALLISON: Mmmm. I really am just looking for love, you know.

Allison walks out and towards the elevator.

ENDRA: (TO HERSELF) Yes, the love that is right in front of you, my dear Allison.

Endra turns, opens the window and motions with her hands for the scent to exit.

ENDRA:

> My dear wind, do carry this scent,
> this special brew,
> Invoke the spaces of the in-between,
> So Allison's love may see the truth,
> And in return, be finally seen.

A gust of wind rattles through the tree outside obliging her request, just as there is a loud tap upon her door.

SCENE 3: AL

AL: Yoo-hoo! Anyone home? Is Miss Endra here?

ENDRA: Yes dear! Do come in.

AL: I learned that from Joe. You know, calling out before you enter. He had the cutest way of doing that, in all kinds of voices.

ENDRA: Who is Joe? Someone I know?

AL: Oh, no. Someone I know. My previous lover who left me. He would come home from work greeting me in the kitchen as Al Pacino. An Al for an Al he used to say. His Pacino was dead on, but his Cher was to die for. Last concert, my ass. My Joe brought her out every night! I miss Cher. (SIGHS) Well, that was Joe. Notice the past tense. That's why I'm here. I'm looking for my next Joe.

ENDRA: Another Joe? (CARRYING THE WATERING CAN OVER TO THE HERB GARDEN)

AL: I loved Joe and I just can't get over him. I hope you can find me my next Joe because Joe doesn't want to have anything to do with me. My friends keep asking me if I am depressed. They think I am in mourning. I told them I just like to wear black. I do miss Joe. Can you help me?

ENDRA: That's a good question, my dear. How about helping me first?

AL: Um, okay. What are you trying to do with that watering can anyway?

Endra points to a large gardenia in a small pot.

ENDRA: Well, I ran out of large pots and I thought this watering can might work for this gardenia instead. Now, why don't you tell me about Joe, while helping me.

AL: Oh, I don't know where to begin. Joe was my whole world. We did everything together. I guess in hindsight, some things about our relationship worked and some things didn't. But I thought we would just find our way through that. Instead, Joe just up and left me and I can't get over him. I want my Joe back. But he doesn't want to get back together. (AL STICKS HIS HAND IN THE DIRT) Gee, I forgot how much fun transplanting could be. I've always loved the feel of dirt through my fingers. So, you really want to transplant that gardenia into this watering can?

ENDRA: Sure. A gardenia can love being in a watering can just as much as a pot. Don't you think?

AL: I would never have thought of putting a gardenia in a watering can. You are so creative Endra.

ENDRA: And yet, look how beautiful the gardenia is in the watering can. Sometimes traditional thought gets you stuck and you're unable to see the truth or imagine anything different. But once you open up to it, beautiful things can bloom.

AL: (TURNING THE WATERING CAN IN HIS HANDS) That's an interesting way to look at it. I've never thought of that. And this gardenia looks amazing bursting out of the top of the can. (SNIFFS) Is that strawberry jam I smell?

ENDRA: (SMILING AND COCKING HER BROW) That's the scent of the gardenia's dried petals. You certainly do have a talent for herbs and potting.

As Endra looks up, a tapestry seems to fall from the ceiling. Embroidered upon it is Al's face and he is holding two potted plants. On the ground beside him are three broken pots. The three pots quickly morph into a man's smiling face. Endra knows him.

AL: I used to do a lot of gardening. My friends called me the Green Giant, because I had the biggest and best herbs and vegetables around. But that was a long time ago. I really should get back into it though, it was fun.

ENDRA: Oh that's a lovely idea and I have the perfect person for you to go see. His name is Henry. He has the best plant shop in town and he will have everything you need. He is just about three blocks up the road, on the left. Tell him Endra sent you.

AL: Okay, I will. It's funny I never saw that shop before. I came over 50 miles to see you Endra, and what a bonus to find a new store with fresh herbs and plants. You know, this gardenia has inspired me. I might just be ready to find my pot of love with someone different. Please don't forget to let me know if you think of anyone.

ENDRA: Of course.

Al bounces down the hallway. Endra stands in the doorway. The elevator bell rings and the door opens.

SCENE 4: KATHERINE

KATHERINE: (EXITS THE ELEVATOR AND SHOUTS) You must be Endra!

Katherine rushes down the hallway.

KATHERINE: I'm not late am I? Oh, I hope you don't mind if I'm late. I don't mind if people are late. I would rather they be early, but I don't mind if they are late. Late or early, both are fine with me.

ENDRA: Why don't you take a seat and tell me what you would like in a man?

KATHERINE: I would prefer a refined man, who has taste and class. But, if you want to know whether or not I am looking for someone who likes the outdoors I would have to say yes. If he likes to binge watch TV shows, that's okay too. Either way works for me. And if he likes to party all hours and go to concerts, that's fun too. Now, I prefer he have dark hair, but blonde is good too. Blonde with dark streaks would be great. But I have to admit, a red head is pretty hot sometimes, too.

ENDRA: That certainly narrows it down.

KATHERINE: Oh, good. Because I guess I really have some specifics, yet I can be flexible too. You know, I really love Latin men. And Europeans are adorable. I saw this documentary once and I could really shack up with a rugged Alaskan. But too far North might be too cold for me, although I do love looking at all that pretty snow. You see, warm weather is really my favorite. And to have a big, tall guy in warm weather just opens up so many possibilities. Although, a short, stocky guy with a great personality would be nice, too. Shy's okay. I hope I am painting a good picture for you?

ENDRA: You certainly are.

A large framed canvas grows around Katherine and hangs in mid-air. Katherine's face stays where it is, her lips continue moving yet Endra hears no words. Endra sees Katherine sitting, meditating by a tree, while a package floats beside her. Three other packages sit untouched on the ground.

ENDRA: (TO HERSELF) Katherine everything is right in front of your face. You just need to make a choice.

The packages dismantle creating the name of a man, in the air.

ENDRA: Oh . . . Louie!

Endra's vision dissolves and she hears Katherine speaking again.

KATHERINE: As you can tell, I know who I am looking for, but who do you think would be good for me?

ENDRA: Louie is your man. He is focused. He is decisive. Your opposite energies will keep you entertained. He loves to travel, to watch TV, to explore different cultures, to go to concerts, to stay home and to go out into the world. He is open minded and willing to act upon many possibilities.

KATHERINE: He sounds wonderful! I'll try him! That was easy, thank you!

Katherine leaves Endra's office.

ENDRA: It will be interesting to see where the two of them end up hanging out! Oh, what a long day. Time to clean up the office and head home.

Endra straightens her office, shuts her appointment book and places her blue book of energy in her purse. She turns off the light, and closes the door behind her.

***

ACT 6

WALKING HOME THROUGH WINDOVER

Endra walks down the block and reaches Henry's Flower Shop. A strong scent stops her in front of the shop and Endra looks in.

ENDRA: Ahh, strawberry jam. That's right, the scent of the gardenia petals, that Al loved. And there he is, in the shop.

Al is grinning and Henry is playfully pushing up against him. They are both in front of a wall of potted plants when Henry leans into Al, and whispers something that makes them both giggle.

ENDRA: (SMILING) The flirting has commenced. And a relationship is all set to bloom.

Walking further, Endra stops

ENDRA: Oh, the scent of magnolia, jasmine and lavender. (ENDRA LOOKS UP AND READS THE SIGN) Chez Jacques. And there is Allison inside. And that well-dressed man must be her date.

A man exits the restaurant, talking on his cellphone. Endra overhears.

MAN WITH CELLPHONE: Hey Steve, I just saw your sister Allison with Chuck. It's about time they went out on a date. Yeah, Chuck said she looked amazing and smelled great. Yeah I guess she's off the market.

Endra smiles and continues to walk.

ENDRA: Ahh, a great day. But tonight is all about me and Knight.

Endra reaches her cottage

***

ACT 7

A NIGHT WITH KNIGHT

Endra enters the hallway. A faint light glows as a dark shadow moves from the candlelight of her bedroom, towards her.

ENDRA: Ahh, Knight. You make my heart skip a beat, darling.

Together they walk into the living room where he stops and places his muscular arms around her waist.

KNIGHT: (LOOKING INTO HER EYES) Ahh, mi inamorata. Let the energy of the day fall away. Now is just for us.

Knight rubs his cheek across her face and kisses her.

ENDRA: And what a day it has been. So many scenes unfolded right in front of my eyes. I had visions all day long.

KNIGHT: (GRINNING) It sounds quite magickal.

Knight steps toward the bookcase, reaches up and grabs something on the shelf.

ENDRA: Knight, what are you reaching for there?

Knight grins, swoops beside Endra and hands her a worn wooden box. On the top is a Fleur de Lys, her ancestors' crest. They walk into the kitchen and Endra sits at the table.

KNIGHT: Perhaps, you should draw some Tarot cards, my dear.

Knight is standing next to Endra as he places his foot on the chair beside her.

ENDRA: A great idea. My cards always help with clarity.

Knight tenderly strokes her hair behind her ear with one hand and flips open the wooden box with the other. He pulls out Tarot cards and hands them to Endra.

KNIGHT: So tell me. What do they say?

Endra holds them in her hands for a few moments, closes her eyes and mixes them.

ENDRA: Okay. If I reflect back on this morning, I can see and hear in my head the angry clouds, the rumbling ground, and the smoldering smoke, the squawking birds, the explosion of the car that backfired, and the spilled coffee.

She draws a card.

ENDRA: The Tower Card, of course. Everything in that card came to life this morning, up until the time I met Alysia.

KNIGHT: (INTIMATELY MASSAGING HER SHOULDERS) The Tower Card. The rapture of Yin and Yang energy at its best. It moves from construction to destruction and back again. Nature balancing itself. It's circular, my dear. But all that has passed. Next?

She picks another card.

ENDRA: The Ace of Cups. Of course, relationships. I had a full day of relationships today, one after the other. This is why jasmine and patchouli greeted me at my office door.

Knight leans in and kisses Endra upon the lips.

KNIGHT: And then?

ENDRA: I had four clients in a row.

Endra draws four Tarot cards and places them alongside the others.

ENDRA: Hmm. The 6 of Cups. The 10 of Cups. The 5 of Cups. The 4 of Cups.

KNIGHT: The 6 of Cups? Your first client was quite the dreamer, trying to plan his adult life. I suppose trying to fit in like everyone else?

Endra leans into Knights chin and laughs.

ENDRA: A perfect description of Glenn. I even saw a scene from his childhood as if it was happening today.

KNIGHT: Hmm. Next?

ENDRA: And the next card, the 10 of Cups, completely describes all the love that was around Allison. And yet she couldn't see what she longed for, which was right in front of her face.

KNIGHT: Not seeing what's right in front of you, it's so simple.

ENDRA: Yes. A potion and a spell showed her and her love that their friendship had grown into the love she sought.

KNIGHT: A special scent for a happy ending, and the 5 of Cups? So, someone was distressed and regretful, and had to be taught how to turn a disappointment into a triumph.

ENDRA: Yes. (LAUGHING) Such a beautiful tapestry bloomed into a new relationship. And in return, Al helped me repot my gardenia to my watering can!

Knight laughs, nibbling her ear.

KNIGHT: You're such a little witch Endra. Just one client left, the 4 of Cups.

ENDRA: Ahh she was easy. Katherine was open to all possibilities. She just needed to focus and enjoy one. She painted quite a picture all around her! All her packages might finally open up.

KNIGHT: A full day of relationships, indeed.

Knight yawns and stretches his arms reaching to the ceiling.

KNIGHT: It appears your cards came to life, right in front of your eyes, all day long! Hmm, might you have a card or two left for this evening?

ENDRA: Of course, my dear.

Folding the rest of the cards into the deck, Endra picks two cards and lays them side by side on the table.

ENDRA: (SMILING) The 2 of Cups and the 3 of Cups.

KNIGHT: (LOOKS AT HER AND COCKS HIS EYEBROW) And what does that mean?

ENDRA: The 2 of Cups is the sign of a perfect match (LOOKS AT KNIGHT WHO SMILES DOWN AT HER) and the 3 of Cups represents joy, celebration and fun.

KNIGHT: Well then maybe we need to honor the cards and go celebrate and have some fun.

Knight picks up Endra in his arms and carries her to the bedroom, where they both disappear. The candles flicker twice and go out, as the Grandfather clock chimes. The cottage remains aglow with the energy of the night.

***

ACT 8

THE BLUE BOOK OF ENERGY

In the living room, upon the same bookcase that had held Endra's Tarot cards, a blue book vibrates on its own. It is Endra's blue book of energy. From inside it a gust of air rumbles the pages back and forth, before the book settles open upon page thirty-one. The following invocation pulses as candlelight flickers on the words around it:

"I have the clarity to know what it is I want and I operate from that."

***

THE END

Endra:
Anecdotes of a
Modern Day Witch

Phase 2:
The Real Practice
of Herbs

by Polonious

ENDRA: ANECDOTES OF A MODERN DAY WITCH

Phase 2 – The Real Practice of Herbs

<u>CAST OF CHARACTERS (in order of appearance):</u>

ENDRA...........................*Energy maven living in Windover.*

STORE OWNER..............*The owner of The Dark Cauldron,*
a New Age Store

JESSICA ....*Young girl, works at*
The Dark Cauldron

ACUPUNCTURIST.........*Regular patron of*
The Dark Cauldron

JONATHAN DEMARCO .*Works in Endra's office building,*
an Attorney

DONALD.........................*Endra's client*

KNIGHT ....*Endra's companion and lover*

<u>SETTINGS IN WINDOVER:</u>

♦*Main Street, Windover*   ♦*The Dark Cauldron*
♦*Endra's Office*   ♦*Endra's Cottage*
♦*Endra's office building*   ♦*Beekeeping area*

Phase 2: The Real Practice of Herbs

ACT 1

ENDRA WALKING DOWN THE STREET

ENDRA: (STOPS SHORT PONDERING) Jars. Hmm, what's this about? I never run low on supplies. But my herbs are ready to be harvested. And I do need jars. (LOOKS UP AND SEES THE SIGN "THE DARK CAULDRON," LAUGHS) What a funny name! I've never noticed this place. But the energy is leading me here. And they'll probably have the jars. So let's see what's brewing!

***

ACT 2

INSIDE "THE DARK CAULDRON"

The Dark Cauldron is a new age shop with canning supplies, bottles, herbs, books, pendulums, jewelry, pentacles, and wands. At the front of the store are two people who appear to be employees and are dressed in black capes and heavy facial makeup, one with a tattoo on her chin.

ENDRA: (JOKINGLY TO HERSELF) My, my it looks like somebody overdosed on the black eye liner today. Let's see, where are those canning supplies?

STORE OWNER: (YELLS FROM THE BACK OF THE STORE) If you need any help, never mind those two. I'm the head witch here.

ENDRA: (SMILING) Of course you are.

Endra continues to peruse the stereotypical items in the store, and can't help but overhear the conversation taking place around her.

STORE OWNER: Oh did you get the benefit of the full moon last night? I used it to charge my wand and I wrote another spell.

JESSICA: Oh I did that too. And I also cast a circle to try to capture the full essence of the negative energy around it.

ENDRA: (TO HERSELF) Negative energy? Casting a circle? Who are these characters?

ACUPUNCTURIST: In my expert opinion you both have excess liver Yang rising. The moon is going to bring in some Yin energy. I can replace that negative energy with positive energy. I should treat the both of you.

ENDRA: (TO HERSELF) Treating people? (SHUDDERS) Who's treating them?

JESSICA: (TALKS LOUDER AS HER EYES DART OVER TO ENDRA) Oh please, treat me, treat me! I need to be treated. I think I have some negative energy around me. And I left my pendulum in the car.

STORE OWNER: Oh, that negative energy is potent and you really have to be careful when you deal with it. I often wake up in the middle of the night calling upon the God and the Goddess as I cast a circle.

Endra rolls her eyes, then looks in their direction, aware that their voices have been getting louder and louder and seem to be directed at her.

ENDRA: (TO HERSELF) Hmm, so many eyes upon me. Why would I be directed to this?

JESSICA: Ooh, don't forget, you have a full schedule of readings and healings today.

STORE OWNER: Yes. That's why we need to finish with this brew.

ACUPUNCTURIST: We have a lot of people depending on us and our herbs. And after you put that coupon out, we've been swamped. You're going to have to actually hire and pay me soon.

JESSICA: I know. Have you noticed our reviews? Everyone keeps commenting how much they need us.

ENDRA: (TO HERSELF) So people believe that they need these characters and their chicken soup to heal? (GROANS) How foolish. We all have what we need. These characters are the only ones who need this.

JESSICA: Maybe I'll feel like you guys after I get certified as a guru. Right now, I just want to eat!

ACUPUNCTURIST: I just want to heal!

STORE OWNER: And I just want to teach and minister to the masses!

ENDRA: (GROANING AND INTERRUPTING) Excuse me! Canning supplies?

STORE OWNER: Oh they are over here on the other side of this archway. But you have to be very careful passing through here. This is a special brew, and, well, you know.

ENDRA: (SHRUGGING OFF THE REPLY, WALKS THROUGH THE THREE OF THEM AND PEEKS

INTO THE CAULDRON) Oh yes I see. You are cooking something.

ENDRA: (UNDER HER BREATH) Looks like chicken noodle.

The three move to the side as Endra confidently walks through the archway.

JESSICA: Hey, what are we doing for lunch?

Endra reaches over and picks up some jars.

ENDRA: Oh are these all the canisters you have?

STORE OWNER: Yes, those are the best money can buy.

Endra shrugs.

ENDRA: This will have to do. My herbs will be fine.

Endra walks back through the archway towards the register. The three women follow her.

JESSICA: What are you going to do with those jars?

STORE OWNER: Of course she is going to use them for herbs. (LOOKS AT ENDRA AND SMIRKS) See these are the novices around me that I have to deal with.

ACUPUNCTURIST: Oh are you an herbalist? Because I'm an herbalist too and I'm an Acupuncturist. I have a special degree and a license.

JESSICA: Oh my God, you guys. I forgot to tell you. My Mom gave me some extra money, so I'm thinking of using it to start my guru certification.

STORE OWNER: Oh, that would be a great certification for you. As a High Priestess, I'm covered for pretty much everything.

Endra places her jars on the counter.

STORE OWNER: (PICKS UP THE JARS AND RINGS THEM UP) We don't see you here often and I have a good sense of people and think you might have some psychic ability. And there's a group of us that get together. You know, the ones who are really psychic. Maybe you'd like to join us?

ENDRA: Energy aligns as it aligns. What is the total for my canning jars please? (SMILES AND PAYS) Enjoy your lunch.

STORE OWNER: Oh dear, my brew!

As Endra leaves, the three rush back to their cauldron as their voices trail off.

ACUPUNCTURIST: It's my brew! We are using my herbs!

JESSICA: Well, I'm the one that put it together. Do you think it needs more papaya? Well anyways, I'm stirring it. It's my wand. Doesn't that make it mine?

STORE OWNER: Hey, it's my store, my cauldron, my brew.

Endra continues walking down the street to her office.

***

ACT 3

ENDRA'S BUILDING

Endra enters the building and directly inside is an attorney's office and a man calls out to her. Endra walks to his office. The door reads "Jonathan DeMarco, Attorney At Law."

ENDRA: Jonathan, nice to see you!

JONATHAN: (GIVES HER A QUICK HUG AND KISS ON THE CHEEK) Hi Endra, it's always nice to see you. Unfortunately today, I need to talk to you about something important. And it's not pleasant.

ENDRA: Oh, okay dear. I was just heading to my office.

JONATHAN: I'll walk with you. We can talk a little more privately in your office.

They reach Endra's office and she opens the door. Jonathan sits down and Endra starts to make tea.

JONATHAN: Endra, as your Legal Representative, I just received this letter from the State Department's Division of Registration.

ENDRA: (LOOKING AT HIM, SHE SHAKES HER HEAD PUZZLED) Tea's almost ready.

JONATHAN: Thank you, Endra. Now this letter is a Cease and Desist Order from the Licensing Division of Matchmakers.

ENDRA: The Licensing Division of Matchmakers?

JONATHAN: Yes. It wants you to cease and desist from your practice. You know, the matchmaking.

ENDRA: Matchmaking? What do you mean my matchmaking practice?

JONATHAN: The law states that you are required to take and pass a class. Jasper Daniels' class certifies you as a legitimate matchmaker.

ENDRA: Who's Jasper Daniels? And a class for matchmakers?

JONATHAN: I'm looking up his website now. Here is what it says. (HOLDS UP HIS IPAD) Jasper Daniels offers affordable, distance learning and is the only Certified Matchmaker Instructor approved by the Board of Matchmakers. (PUTS HIS IPAD DOWN AND LOOKS AT ENDRA)

ENDRA: (HEARTILY LAUGHS) Jonathan, that's rubbish! This has to be some kind of a joke.

JONATHAN: This isn't a joke. There was a precedent set.

ENDRA: A precedent?

JONATHAN: Yes. A precedent. If you do the work of a matchmaker you are required to follow the rules set by the government, for matchmakers.

ENDRA: So what do they want?

JONATHAN: Let me explain it in a different way. Three years ago, there was a man who distributed herbs and claimed himself to be a healer. In fact, he called himself a shaman.

ENDRA: (WITH SARCASM) Oh, so if a gifted healer wants to use his gift, he also has to take Jasper Daniels' class and become certified? Please Jonathan, what is it they want?

JONATHAN: Yes, well in this case the man did. The Licensing Board wanted to see his credentials: where he went to school, was it a Board approved school, did he take all his licensing tests and pay all his fees.

ENDRA: Ahh. So they are looking for money.

JONATHAN: As long as he paid his fees, took some classes and subscribed to the Board's rules, they allowed him to call himself a shaman.

ENDRA: They allowed?

JONATHAN: Funny thing is, this man made more money building peoples' websites than from any shaman work. Yet because he called himself a shaman, he was required to follow the licensing rules.

ENDRA: Shaman? I haven't seen any evidence of a shaman walking on these streets. People building websites, well, there are plenty of them.

JONATHAN: Well, that was just my example. But this same precedent has been set for matchmakers. And you are required by law to follow it.

ENDRA: So, this is a game of follow the leader. What do we do to get rid of this annoyance?

JONATHAN: Endra, it's just a formality and we can deal with it very easily.

ENDRA: What are you thinking Jonathan?

JONATHAN: Here's what I'm thinking. This Cease and Desist Order came from a group of local matchmakers who filed complaints that you were practicing without a license. I believe these matchmakers who have joined together are not as successful as you and want you to stop practicing.

ENDRA: They want me to stop practicing?

JONATHAN: Yes. I think it's clear you are a threat to them. And they were clever enough to find a precedent to hang their hat on.

ENDRA: What a pack of mules. Well my dear Jonathan, I'm not going to stop anything that I do.

JONATHAN: Endra, all you need to do is take the class and pass it. Once you do that, you will be certified, and then you just have to pay the fees to the state. You will then be in compliance and can continue with what you are doing. Otherwise you can't keep doing your matchmaking.

ENDRA: Jonathan, I will continue to do what I do. How *they* define me or what *they* call me is irrelevant.

Endra looks at Jonathan and he stares back pleading for an answer.

ENDRA: I am not a matchmaker.

JONATHAN: What?

ENDRA: I don't make matches. I align energy and collaborate with it.

JONATHAN: Well . . .

ENDRA: Jonathan, I have never called myself a matchmaker.

JONATHAN: Okay, Endra. This is what our response will be. One, you are not a matchmaker, and you don't hold yourself out to be one. Two, we'll call you an Energy Collaborator. How does that sound?

ENDRA: It sounds fine to me, call me whatever works. It doesn't change what I do.

JONATHAN: Okay. So then, three, you are not required to take any classes or get any certification. I think this is a satisfactory response. And I'll get right to it.

Jonathan leaves Endra's office.

***

ACT 4

DONALD

There is a knock on Endra's door.

ENDRA: Come in!

DONALD: (WITH A BRITISH ACCENT) Cheers! You must be Endra, I'm Donald. (POINTING TO HER TEACUP) Oh I would love a spot of tea, if it isn't a bother?

ENDRA: (COCKS HER BROW AND GETS UP) A spot of tea? Certainly. Are you from across the pond?

DONALD: Well I just flew in from London a few days ago.

ENDRA: Oh are you British?

DONALD: Well . . . no.

ENDRA: So I'm confused. Your British accent?

DONALD: Oh, it's a souvenir. A sort of gift to myself.

ENDRA: A gift to yourself?

DONALD: Yes, I'm really from the South.

ENDRA: And the accent?

DONALD: Well the Tennessee drawl doesn't attract many ladies for me. When I first visited England 10 years ago, I adopted their accent. I love it and the ladies seemed to love it too!

ENDRA: If you have the accent, and the ladies love it, then why are you here?

DONALD: The accent doesn't seem to be working anymore.

ENDRA: Maybe you should be more authentic. Accents can be fun afterwards. Really, Donald, if you can't be yourself, there is nothing I can help you with.

DONALD: (REVERTS TO HIS SOUTHERN DRAWL) Well when I talk to the women in this way I just don't get the same pickins.

ENDRA: Do you really think it's the accent that affects the pickins?

DONALD: Yes . . . or at least I thought so. (WITH HUMILITY) I just really want to go on a date.

ENDRA: A date? Well who would I be setting up? The British you or the *pickins* you?

DONALD: Whatever works Endra. I'm pretty lonely and would love to meet somebody special.

ENDRA: Do you think you could accentuate *the you* first?

DONALD: Hmm. That's a great play on words. If you think I should do that then I will.

ENDRA: Let me think . . . there's Wendy Chou. She is a southern California girl but she likes when people think that she is from China.

DONALD: She sounds like a hoot!

ENDRA: She is a comedian. And she likes to have fun with that. But when she's home, she's just herself. Can you be yourself?

DONALD: I can surely try.

ENDRA: I would suggest that you be nothing more than yourself. Because if you are nothing more than yourself, you will have nothing to apologize for later.

DONALD: I'll give it a shot. Thanks Endra, I'll let you know how it goes.

There's a knock on the door.

ENDRA: Donald, keep me updated.

Donald leaves and Jonathan enters.

JONATHAN: Endra, I sent in your rebuttal and got a response.

ENDRA: More tea Jonathan?

JONATHAN: (SMILES) No Endra, thank you. This is really important.

ENDRA: Ok Jonathan, you have my attention.

JONATHAN: I filed the paperwork. And it is all cleared. But, there are a few things you need to be aware of.

ENDRA: Go on.

JONATHAN: First of all, you are not allowed to use the word 'date.'

ENDRA: I'm not allowed? What if I need to ask someone at the bank what today's date is to deposit all my earnings? Does that mean I'm in trouble?

JONATHAN: Not that date. A 'date' date. I mean, here's the question you need to answer. If you are not setting people up on a date, what are you doing?

ENDRA: I do what I do, Jonathan. I don't care how anyone defines it.

JONATHAN: Well if you aren't setting up people on dates and you are not a matchmaker, but an Energy Collaborator, then you shouldn't be using the word 'date.'

ENDRA: So is their goal to limit the words I use? And if I strike the word date from my vocabulary, then everything is fine? These people got together to limit my vocabulary?

JONATHAN: Well the Licensing Board wants to make sure that you don't practice matchmaking. Or they will shut you down. They feel that if they restrict you from using the word 'date,' then in their minds, that is sufficient.

ENDRA: (WITH SARCASM) You are telling me that if I don't use certain words I can continue doing what I have been doing?

JONATHAN: Well to them, if you don't use the word date then that proves that you are not a matchmaker. (HESITATES) This is ludicrous. You know what, Endra, I have one more idea. Let me get back to you.

Jonathan leaves.

***

ACT 5

ENDRA'S OFFICE

Hours later, Jonathan knocks on Endra's door.

JONATHAN: Do you have a moment? I have some answers.

ENDRA: Sure Jonathan. How distracting all this is and such a waste of our time.

JONATHAN: Here's the gist Endra. The same group of matchmakers that came together also commissioned the Governor to require matchmakers to follow certain rules and pay a fee to practice matchmaking. These same people are now upset that you are making a lot of money as a matchmaker and not following their rules or paying their fees.

ENDRA: This doesn't make sense, Jonathan. This is detail dribble. I am actually helping people. Isn't that what's most important?

JONATHAN: We did win something. You no longer have to take Jasper Daniels' class or pass it. But these people aren't going to forsake their money. You still have to play by their rules.

ENDRA: Oh, I get it. This isn't about helping people. This is about helping a certain few people.

JONATHAN: These people want their $500 fee to register you and they are going to want $500 every two years from you so you can continue doing what you are already doing. Whether you are successful or not doesn't matter to them. They just want their fee. They are trying to exercise their legal advantage over you. So Endra, basically if you pay the $500 we can make this whole thing go away.

ENDRA: (PULLS OUT $500 IN CASH, FROM HER DESK, AND HANDS IT TO JONATHAN) Jonathan, pay them and clear this up.

JONATHAN: I'm sorry Endra. I know this is very frustrating. But this is the fastest and easiest way to keep these people quiet. And you know, now you can use any words you want.

***

ACT 6

ENDRA'S COTTAGE

SCENE 1: ENDRA AND KNIGHT

Later that night at Endra's cottage, she is sitting at her garden table, sipping on her mead wine, talking to Knight as he works with the bees. Knight is not wearing any protective garb or special equipment.

ENDRA: (FLIRTING) So true, my love. That's quite divine.

KNIGHT: I suppose the people out there would call me a Beekeeper. But I don't keep bees. I work with bees and they work with me. They bring me honey, and I am grateful to use their beeswax and I make mead from what they give me. In return I give them real estate. My energy enhances it. They call it beekeeping, but that's just their definition, not mine.

ENDRA: Why do they make definitions for everything? Don't they realize how confining they are?

KNIGHT: Exactly, my dear.

SCENE 2: ENDRA AND HER CAULDRON

Endra goes inside her cottage, picks up her cauldron and places it by her fireplace.

ENDRA: (STARTS FILLING THE CAULDRON)

With water so gently warmed
by the light and energy of the sun,
I fill this cauldron, and mix in these herbs
for this cease and desist distraction to be done.

ENDRA: (THROWS IN PINE)

Pine, as you garnish the mighty forest
with your clean, forceful scent,
Your needles now push away
any one from my space
holding malicious intent.

46

ENDRA: (PICKS UP SAGE, CIRCLES IT AROUND HER
AND DROPS IT IN THE CAULDRON)

> Sage cleanse the energy
> at each time and place,
> And clear all intention
> directed to my space.

ENDRA: (PICKS UP A ROSE, SLOWLY REMOVES
PETALS AND DROPS THEM FROM ABOVE HER
HEAD)

> Beautiful rose full of desire
> as you fall from high above,
> Surround my presence and being everywhere,
> with the totality of love.

ENDRA: (PICKS UP BRANCH FROM APPLE TREE
AND STIRS)

> To a scent, rich in power,
> I mix these herbs with help from you, apple tree.
> Steer these collaborating energies
> to dissolve enemies and injustice,
> setting harmony and goodwill bountifully free!

ENDRA: (WITH GLAZED EYES, ENDRA FOCUSES
INTENTLY)

> What defines me and who I am
> is never based upon what I do,
> What, how and who I surround myself with
> is the true picture of me,
> created for all of you!

*Endra extends her hands outward into the space and air
around her. The scent powerfully travels outside to Knight
and quickly consumes further beyond.*

Knight flows into the cottage, scoops Endra in his arms and gently kisses her.

***

ACT 7

ENDRA'S OFFICE

It is the next day at Endra's office and Jonathan comes in.

ENDRA: Good morning Jonathan.

JONATHAN: Hey, here's your $500 back. That committee of matchmakers causing you problems has dissolved. (JONATHAN SHAKES HEAD) Yeah, dissolved. Funny story . . .

JONATHAN: This new company sprouted out of the internet. It's called DeservingLove.com. It's a new matchmaking website which allows people who are looking for dates to join for free. It is the latest craze. In response, all the local matchmakers are going out of business. They are now more concerned about themselves and their own livelihood so the group has disbanded. Good news for you, I'm giving you your money back and they are out of your hair. On the flip side I hope that internet craze doesn't negatively impact your business. Because you know, Endra, all those matchmakers have lost their shirts.

ENDRA: Don't worry about me, Jonathan. Alysia constantly finds new blouses for me. (WITH WIT) And besides, I'm an Energy Collaborator, remember?

***

ACT 8

THE BLUE BOOK OF ENERGY

That night, back in Endra's garden, amongst her herbs, a wind blows through the trees and opens Endra's blue book of energy. The book settles open on page fifty-eight. The following invocation pulses as candlelight flickers on the words around it:

"I define the expression of my true nature."

***

THE END

Endra: Anecdotes of a Modern Day Witch

Phase 3: Time for Reiki

By
Polonious

ENDRA: ANECDOTES OF A MODERN DAY WITCH

Phase 3 – Time for Reiki

<u>CAST OF CHARACTERS (in order of appearance):</u>

ENDRA.........................*Energy maven living in Windover.*
KNIGHT ....*Endra's companion and lover*
MAN ON STREET.......*Young man with blood on him*
DYING WOMAN ....*Woman dying in bed in hospital*
MALE VOICE ....*Distant male voice in hospital room*
WOMAN ON STREET *Woman lying on street, struck by car*
SPECTATOR 1.............*Random spectator on the street*
SPECTATOR 2.............*Random spectator on the street*
SPECTATOR 3.............*Random spectator on the street*
SPECTATOR 4.............*Random spectator on the street*
SPECTATOR 5.............*Random spectator on the street*
ALYSIA........................*Works in Endra's office building,
                                           fashion designer*
JONATHAN ....*Works in Endra's office building,
                                           an Attorney*
BRYAN.........................*Young man from accident,
                                           Endra's Client*

EXTRAS ....*Various people crowding in the
                                           streets.*

<u>SETTINGS IN WINDOVER:</u>

♦*Main Street, Windover*   ♦*Random Hospital Room*
♦*Endra's Office*   ♦*Small family home*
♦*Endra's Cottage*

Phase 3: Time for Reiki

ACT 1

NIGHTTIME IN WINDOVER

SCENE 1: ALONG MAIN STREET

There is a full moon and Endra and Knight are walking hand in hand along Main Street.

ENDRA: Dinner was great tonight. And your mead left me a little woozy. I can't resist your vanilla and cardamom elixir. We always have a great time together, Knight.

KNIGHT: (KISSING HER NECK AND WHISPERING IN HER EAR) My sentiments exactly, mi inamorata.

ENDRA: Oh that feels wonderful. I wish you could stop time so I could enjoy this moment, forever.

KNIGHT: Your wish is my command, darling. You know I handle time differently.

ENDRA: Hmm. Well I have many more wishes, my love. If you have the time . . .

KNIGHT: (LAUGHS DEEPLY) If I have the time? It's wonderful that time moves in a different way for me. Past, present and future are all at my command. For you my dear, I have all the time in the world.

ENDRA: Let's pick up the pace then. I'd like to get home and well . . . spend our time together there.

KNIGHT: (LAUGHS) I'll gladly drive your chariot, my love . . .

ENDRA: And I'll gladly climb aboard!

Just then a screech of wheels and a loud bang occurs.

ENDRA: What was that?

KNIGHT: (GRABS ENDRA'S HAND TIGHTER, AND PUTS HIS ARM AROUND HER) Let's walk further to find out.

Endra and Knight continue to walk briskly to the corner, in the direction of the noise. A man with blood on him, who seems a little shaken, quickly passes by them.

ENDRA: (LOOKS TOWARDS THE MAN AND GRABS KNIGHT'S ARM) Oh my! Did you see the look on his face?

KNIGHT: Yes, he's heading down the street in that direction.

ENDRA: Yes. That's strange. Because back that way is the crowd. (POINTS IN THE OPPOSITE DIRECTION)

Endra and Knight head towards the crowd when they both stop and look at each other. Everything goes dark as they are transported to another place and time.

SCENE 2: HOSPITAL BED, BACK IN TIME

Endra and Knight are standing at the foot of the bed of a young woman.

ENDRA: Knight do you know where we are? Look at this poor woman. She's so pale, and barely breathing.

KNIGHT: I'm not sure where we are but I know this is related to whatever is going on with that man who was running down the street.

Endra looks at him with big eyes.

KNIGHT: Don't forget Endra, we are here together.

ENDRA: I know. It looks like she is dying.

Knight nods his head in agreement.

MALE VOICE: (IN THE DISTANCE) I'm not sure she's going to make it. I've done all I can. This is so difficult for me.

ENDRA: Oh, she is dying. That must be the doctor speaking.

Knight grabs her hand as the room goes out of focus again.

SCENE 3: BACK IN THE PRESENT, NIGHTTIME IN WINDOVER

Things come back into focus and Endra and Knight find themselves back on the street heading towards the crowd. There is a woman lying in the middle of the street with a car stopped behind her.

ENDRA: (TO KNIGHT) Oh no, I think she just got hit by that car.

An ambulance siren blares as it gets closer. Endra and Knight overhear people in the crowd.

SPECTATOR 1: How did he do that?

SPECTATOR 2: Who was that young man?

SPECTATOR 3: Is he a doctor? No way he could be a doctor!

SPECTATOR 4: He's no doctor.

SPECTATOR 1: Where did he go?

SPECTATOR 2: I don't know?

SPECTATOR 3: I don't know either but he saved her life.

SPECTATOR 4: He gave her CPR. Why did he run away?

SPECTATOR 5: What just happened? I think he just saved her life.

KNIGHT: (TO ENDRA) Well, there's nothing we can do. The ambulance just pulled up.

Knight pulls Endra closer as they walk away towards her home.

ENDRA: That man we saw running had something to do with this, but I don't know what.

KNIGHT: But we do know somehow that it is related to that woman in the hospital bed.

ENDRA: I'm not sure what to do with all of this. Why are we seeing it?

KNIGHT: Maybe there is nothing for us to do with this at the moment. When the time comes for us to do something, we will know and we can do it then.

ENDRA: Well for now, let's just send some Reiki energy to the young man and the woman.

Endra and Knight enter her cottage.

***

ACT 2

THE NEXT DAY

SCENE 1: ENDRA'S OFFICE BUILDING

Endra enters the building and sees Alysia, who quickly approaches.

ALYSIA: Hey, good morning Endra, how are you?

JONATHAN: (PASSING BY) Good morning ladies!

ALYSIA: Good morning Jonathan!

ENDRA: Good morning!

ALYSIA: Endra, I hope you don't mind but I have someone I was hoping you could see first thing this morning. I met this guy the other night, he is new in town, and he seems like a very nice guy. I think he just needs to meet some new people. He seems a little preoccupied and you are good at getting people to open up.

ENDRA: (SMILING) Alysia, of course I will do that for you. If I can help a friend of yours, I am happy to.

ALYSIA: Oh, I'm so glad you said that because I told him to head up to your office.

ENDRA: Now?

ALYSIA: Yes! He's up there now. I let him in and told him to wait for you. I didn't think you would mind.

ENDRA: Okay Alysia, let me see what I can do.

Endra walks towards her office and once alone she stops short.

ENDRA: Knight? You are here with me? Okay. Darling, is there a reason you are here?

Endra continues to walk and reaches her office. She sees the man sitting in her office.

ENDRA: Oh, my goodness, it's the same young man from the accident, Knight. Knowing you are here reassures me that there is a reason in time for this. You are a part of this too. (LOOKS AT THE MAN, AND WALKS TOWARDS HIM) Hello, I'm Endra. It is a pleasure to meet you. And you are?

BRYAN: My name is Bryan.

Endra looks down and notices her watch has stopped. At the same time she feels Knight by her side and everything becomes unfocused. The scene goes dark.

SCENE 2: HOSPITAL BED, BACK IN TIME

Endra and Knight are once again standing at the foot of the bed of a young woman. This time the door of the room opens and a man wearing a white coat comes in and walks to the front of the bed. His face is hidden.

MALE VOICE: (TO HIMSELF) I'm not sure she's going to make it. I've done all I can. This is so difficult for me. (TURNS TO FACE ENDRA AND KNIGHT)

Endra gasps as she grabs Knight's hand tighter.

ENDRA: His face. He's the same young man who ran past us the other night!

MALE VOICE: Oh, my dear. (WALKING OVER TO THE WOMAN'S BEDSIDE) I don't know what else I can do. What kind of a doctor am I? (FIGHTING BACK TEARS) I've tried every procedure I know.

ENDRA: (MOVES CLOSER TO KNIGHT) And he's the same young man waiting in my office, right now!

Knight takes Endra's hand and they walk out of the hospital room. They are suddenly in a small family home. Knight points to the family crest on the wall and they both glance from one picture to the next.

ENDRA: (LOOKING AT KNIGHT) Oh my God! He is not just her doctor, he's her brother.

The Doctor/Bryan is sitting in a chair, by himself in the house, sobbing.

KNIGHT: He is devastated over this. He can't get over that he couldn't save her.

Everything comes back into focus for Endra. She notices her watch begins to move and she is suddenly back in her office.

ENDRA: (EXTENDING HER HAND) Oh, it's nice to meet you Bryan.

SCENE 3: ENDRA'S OFFICE

BRYAN: Are you sure you have the time to talk right now?

ENDRA: Yes. Of course I do.

BRYAN: You know Endra, I am feeling a little bit lost. It just feels like something in my life is unresolved. I'm kind of in a fog.

ENDRA: How can I help you?

BRYAN: By a stroke of luck, I met Alysia and I was telling her how I felt. She said maybe I just need to get out more and meet more people.

ENDRA: Sometimes that helps.

BRYAN: Alysia said a lot of people in Windover are really nice. So I thought I should at least give it a try. She said you would be the best person to help me with that.

ENDRA: Yes. Alysia is a nice person.

BRYAN: Maybe she's right, and I just need to meet more people. What do you think Endra?

As the sun hits her arm, Endra glances out her open window.

ENDRA: Sure. Let's see if we can work this out.

Suddenly a bird flies in through her open window. It flies in a circle around and around Endra's office, then hits the mirror and falls to the floor.

BRYAN: (JUMPS UP STARTLED) Geez, what was that?

Bryan walks towards the bird as Endra moves slowly in the same direction, standing behind him.

BRYAN: Oh gosh, it's just a little bird. And she's hurt. (PICKS THE BIRD UP IN HIS HANDS)

ENDRA: Carry her over to my desk. I've put a towel down.

Bryan gently places the bird on her desk.

BRYAN: She's moving. It looks like she's breathing. She must be stunned.

ENDRA: I think you are right.

BRYAN: (LOOKING AT THE BIRD'S WINGS) It looks like her wings are fine, her beak looks okay and her head. I don't see any signs of trauma or injury.

ENDRA: Gee you seem to have a very good medical knowledge. Or perhaps, a good knowledge of birds?

BRYAN: (LAUGHS) Birds . . . Hah! I don't know anything about birds. But she does need some help, and if I can help her, I should, shouldn't I?

ENDRA: Well what are you proposing to do for the bird?

BRYAN: I feel like there is something I should be doing for her. To help her.

ENDRA: Right now it looks like the bird is healing on its own. And we are helping just by being here and giving the bird that space, and our energies. We took the bird out of harm's way and there's nothing more we can do.

BRYAN: (LOOKS BACK AND FORTH FROM THE BIRD TO ENDRA) If there was something I could do I'd do it, but I suppose there isn't.

ENDRA: It seems we've done all we can for the bird. The bird has to heal all on its own or not.

BRYAN: There is something about this whole thing that doesn't make sense. It's like there is something inside me that feels it could do more for the bird.

ENDRA: What do you think? Should we get some ice for it, maybe figure out some way to make a splint, or maybe it needs some water when it wakes up?

BRYAN: Ooh, I don't know if any of those things will help. I mean, it looks like it's kind of resting.

ENDRA: How so?

BRYAN: I don't know. But it looks kind of comfortable healing, right here with us. Maybe there isn't anything else for me to do. Hmm. That's a different feeling for me. I always feel like there is something more I should do when something like this occurs.

ENDRA: Go on.

BRYAN: Well, I don't know. I feel like there is something significant about having this medical knowledge yet I don't know where it comes from. Since I have no formal training nobody listens to me so it makes this feeling even more difficult to deal with. Then I end up doing nothing or something less than what I know I could do.

ENDRA: So, do you believe that by not doing anything, you are actually doing nothing?

BRYAN: Well this time it feels different. There's really nothing to do. And I'm not sure what to do with that.

ENDRA: Oh. So not doing what you have always done with that feeling is doing something new, isn't it, my dear?

BRYAN: Ha! Ha! That would make sense.

ENDRA: It sounds like you have started to do something different already. You must be on the right path.

BRYAN: (WALKING OVER TO THE WINDOW) Well it's just the beginning, I guess.

ENDRA: And that's a start, isn't it? Now, shall we figure out where you could meet some people?

BRYAN: You know Endra, right now, I don't think I want to meet anyone. I think I would like to get to know myself, me, who I am, a bit better, first.

Bryan walks over and hugs Endra.

BRYAN: I'm not sure where I am going with this but I do feel a lot better. Thank you, Endra.

ENDRA: And in feeling better, you shall find a greater joy in being you, Bryan.

Endra walks over to the door with Bryan and he leaves. Closing the door and turning around, she sees the bird start to stir, get on its feet and fly directly out the window.

ENDRA: Thank you dear! (WAVES HER HAND AFTER THE BIRD)

***

ACT 3

IN THE GARDEN OF ENDRA'S COTTAGE

Endra and Knight are sitting at a table in their garden eating dinner.

ENDRA: You know Knight, I am constantly amazed at how resilient time is.

KNIGHT: How so, my dear?

ENDRA: Time seems to follow us. Our thoughts, our actions, our habits.

KNIGHT: That's because it is manmade. Man follows time. Yet when you journey beside time and not in it, you are able to see something that others aren't able to see.

ENDRA: Like we were able to see the Doctor with his sister, from a time ago, and how it affected the young man, last night, in the street.

KNIGHT: Yes, for time helps man express himself at different points, in different locations. Time helps man know that he exists and it is the fuel of his movement.

ENDRA: And today, I worked with the man that we saw, in our vision, who was caught in his own structure of time.

KNIGHT: Yes, time is part of our existence until we get out of it. Funny, if you don't get restrained by time, everything works itself out.

ENDRA: Yes, as it did today. The poor dear was locked in a loop which caused him to be trapped in one time. And that carried forward, with him.

KNIGHT: Ahh . . . going back and forth so many times can confuse you as to where you truly are. It can entrap you forcing you to continuously go back to retrieve something.

ENDRA: His thoughts, his actions, his habits followed him. Here.

KNIGHT: Yet, as time exists all at once, darling, you realize you helped more than one today. The man who came to your office and the doctor.

ENDRA: Yes, I know, dear. The fact that I helped Bryan, I helped the doctor. And since I helped the doctor, I helped Bryan.

KNIGHT: Yes, what comes forward from the past, for him, has already been changed. The facts might not change but his understanding and what he carries forward from it can change.

Knight and Endra embrace and they retire for the evening.

***

ACT 4

THE BLUE BOOK OF ENERGY

Back in Endra's kitchen, Endra's blue book of energy opens. The book settles open on page one hundred forty-one. The following invocation pulses as candlelight flickers on the words around it:

"All I am is this exact moment, and in this exact moment, all is well."

***

THE END

Endra: Anecdotes of a Modern Day Witch

Phase 4: Acupressure for Change

 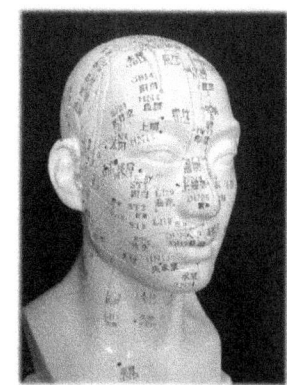

by Polonious

ENDRA: ANECDOTES OF A MODERN DAY WITCH

Phase 4 – Acupressure for Change

CAST OF CHARACTERS (in order of appearance):

ENDRA ....*Energy maven living in Windover.*
SISTER ROBERTA......*Busybody nun*
SISTER NANCY ....*Older nun*
SISTER SALLY ....*Younger nun*
MARY ANNE ....*Department store clerk*
ALYSIA ....*Works in Endra's office building, fashion designer*
PAULIE ABRUZZI ......*Endra's Client*
DELIVERY WOMAN..*Delivery woman*
MAN FROM OFFICE ..*Man from Paulie Abruzzi's office*
KNIGHT ....*Endra's companion and lover*

EXTRAS ....*Random patrons eating at the Lunch Emporium and random customers at Maxmart Department store.*

SETTINGS IN WINDOVER:

♦*Windover Lunch Emporium*   ♦*Endra's Office*
♦*Maxmart Department Store*   ♦*Endra's office building*
♦*Endra's Garden*   ♦*Endra's Cottage*

Phase 4: Acupressure for Change

ACT 1

LUNCH EMPORIUM IN WINDOVER

Endra is at the Lunch Emporium. It is bustling with a lot of people talking loudly and eating. Endra walks with her tray of food to a table and sits down. She places her napkin on her lap and starts to eat. Three nuns are sitting at the table next to hers and she overhears their conversation.

SISTER ROBERTA: (PLACES HER HAND ACROSS HER CHEST) We are blessed to have such a large celebration for your Golden Jubilee tonight, Sister Nancy. How fortunate it is that we were all able to work so hard for you.

SISTER NANCY: Yes and . . .

SISTER ROBERTA: Oh yes, 50 years. How wonderful. So many years and we have all aged, well some of us have. So many sisters are getting up there in age, you both, too. God willing, some of us (PLACES HAND ON CHEST) do show it better than others. But right now we really need to focus on eating. I am really hungry because with Jesus's help we accomplished a lot today. So let's look. They have chicken, vegetables, even fish.

SISTER NANCY: Oh, we mustn't forget! We need to get a piece of fish tonight for our honorary sister, Nora.

SISTER SALLY: Oh, I will make a note of that Sister so we don't forget before we leave.

SISTER ROBERTA: Oh, yes, fish. Perhaps fish would be nice right now. Yes, I could go for a piece of fish.

SISTER NANCY: Oh yes, a piece of fish sounds wonderful Sister. I wouldn't mind sharing that with you. And we could pick up Nora's as well right now.

SISTER ROBERTA: Oh heaven's what a marvelous idea Sister Nancy. You have a big night ahead of you. Perhaps sharing will not be enough. God love you, you'll need your strength. So let's get a piece of fish each. But as for Nora's piece of fish, that's for later on. We don't need to worry about that now. Let's just eat. So what are you thinking of ordering, Sister Sally?

SISTER SALLY: Oh, I thought maybe I would get a light salad.

SISTER ROBERTA: A salad! Sister Sally. Oh my, that wouldn't fill me up. You know we have been working really hard today, moving boxes and furniture. And the other nuns, well we didn't ask them to help us. We could have but we did it all ourselves. You know Sister Nancy you really should be getting all the nuns to help us. And it would be good exercise for them. God bless them.

SISTER NANCY: (PUTS UP HER FINGER IN THOUGHT) You know . . .

SISTER ROBERTA: You know we really should be working as a team. Yet the other sisters are getting older and they really can't make it down to the office any more. That reminds me, where was Sister Pauline? How unfortunate it is that she was unable to join us in the preparation for your special night Sister Nancy. How is Sister Pauline anyway? Did you ever get to visit with her Sister Sally?

SISTER SALLY: Well, Sister Pauline . . .

SISTER ROBERTA: Well let me tell you something about Sister Pauline. (POINTING HER FINGER) She says her prayers every day and she smiles and will tell you that you are a sweet little dear, but deep down that is not what she is really thinking.

SISTER NANCY: Sister Roberta!

SISTER ROBERTA: Well I'm just telling it like it is. And God bless her because she tries very hard. You know sometimes it can be difficult trying to get all this work done. And you don't always get the support you expect. Bless Sister Pauline's little heart. Wouldn't it be nice to get a little bit more support from the sisters? I pray for them, they are old but . . . now for me I am always thinking of everyone else. Sister Nancy, you know I have been there from day one with you and no one can say that I haven't done my fair share. And let's say what a fair share it has been. I'm not saying that we don't all have our little sins that we try to work out. Sister Pauline does always seem to try . . .

Endra having overheard the whole conversation raises her head and looks over at the nuns. She notices the other nuns seem to shy away from the conversation, uncomfortably. The talkative nun is oblivious to everything else except her own voice, her own words.

ENDRA: (TO HERSELF) Okay energy, you got my attention. People almost never speak the truth of the situation. But energy does. So if we are going to flood the space with untruths, then let's have it all come out.

Endra focuses on the Sister's mouth, with the intention that her gossip continues and continues without hesitation as if to exhaust the nun, and clear the space.

ENDRA: And . . . (GESTURING WITH HER HAND)

SISTER ROBERTA: (CONTINUING) Don't you think so Sister Nancy? Because you know it has been 50 years since we took our vows? And oh what a blessed time that was, wasn't it? But for you Sister Sally, you started a little later, so your vows were later than ours. God loves you, and you are getting there.

ENDRA: (LOOKING AT SISTER ROBERTA'S MOUTH, NODS HER HEAD UP AND DOWN) And . . .

SISTER ROBERTA: (CONTINUING) But we do need to think about our food because we worked so hard today. Now if we are all having fish tonight it's better we don't have it now. Let's save that for our special celebration for you Sister Nancy. Are you excited Sister Nancy? Because I'm excited. After all, my Jubilee is coming up right after yours and I am sure it will be a huge celebration because all the sisters love celebrating with me. (BEGINS COUGHING, AND IS OUT OF BREATH)

ENDRA: (LOOKS OVER AND RUBS HER THROAT) And . . .

Sister Roberta continues coughing while trying to talk and puts her index finger up to gesture one moment.

SISTER SALLY: (OFFERING HER A GLASS) Have some water Sister, oh my . . .

SISTER ROBERTA: (TAKES THE WATER) Oh bless you dear.

SISTER NANCY: Are you okay Sister?

Sister Roberta finishes the water and puts the glass down.

SISTER ROBERTA: (STRUGGLING TO SPEAK) Oh, I think so, God willing.

SISTER NANCY: Perhaps we should go up and get our food.

Sister Roberta nods her head, unable to talk.

Endra picks up her tray, empties her trash and walks out of the Lunch Emporium.

ENDRA: Ahh . . . all may not be what it seems for today. Yet it will be a blessed day indeed!

***

ACT 2

DEPARTMENT STORE

Endra enters Maxmart department store. Endra walks up to the service desk and puts a plastic bag on the counter. A short, stocky, 60 year old woman, holding her left shoulder, is rotating her neck.

MARY ANNE: (SNEARS OVER HER GLASSES, WITH A FROZEN SMILE AND SAYS WITH NO EMOTION) How may I help you?

ENDRA: My friend bought these shoes two days ago, wore them once and the heel broke, so I'd like to get her money back.

MARY ANNE: Wait, did you say they've been worn? Can't do it. Store policy doesn't allow you to return used items.

ENDRA: I'm returning them because they are defective.

MARY ANNE: We can't take them back. But you know, a little glue is probably all they need. A little super glue will fix anything, you know.

ENDRA: What? Glue on shoes?

Endra notices Mary Anne wincing in pain while holding her left shoulder. Endra stares at Mary Anne's painful shoulder and touches her own left shoulder, and keeps her hand there.

MARY ANNE: (CRUXES HER NECK BACK AND FORTH AND SAYS TO HERSELF) Hmm, that's a little better.

ENDRA: (LEANS IN) So what can we do about this?

MARY ANNE: Oh, don't worry about store policy in this situation. I'm going to handle this and put this through and return them for you.

ENDRA: (SMILES) Of course you will.

MARY ANNE: The store has policies but I can do whatever I want here. It's my choice whether or not I give discounts or accept returns.

ENDRA: So you control who gets their money back or not?

MARY ANNE: Sure, but don't worry honey, I like you so I will process this for you.

ENDRA: (TAKES THE CASH AND SAYS TO HERSELF) She has no control over anything, least of all, resources.

Endra shakes her head, as she continues to rub her shoulder.

MARY ANNE: 'Cause you know, I have to live by other policies in other stores so why shouldn't people who come in here have to live by the policies that I choose to enforce.

ENDRA: (TO HERSELF) Thanks energy for making this trip short and sweet.

Endra looks at Mary Anne and takes her hand off her shoulder, waves, and exits the store.

MARY ANNE: (MOVING HER NECK) Damn, that pain is coming back.

***

ACT 3

AT ENDRA'S OFFICE BUILDING

Endra arrives at her office building and heads to Alysia's design studio.

ENDRA: (HOLDING MONEY IN THE AIR) Alysia my dear, here's your money!

ALYSIA: What? Oh thank you. I appreciate you doing that. I never get anywhere with those people. Personally, I think they are all passive aggressive, or maybe . . . (WITH A SMIRK) they just don't like me.

ENDRA: No, they don't like anybody there. How can they when everybody is in charge? They decide and feel like they have control. I don't know how you can shop there.

ALYSIA: I actually bought the shoes when a friend told me that the store was donating the proceeds to a charity that she was sponsoring. I got the shoes just to be supportive. I never go to that store otherwise.

ENDRA: It's never comfortable when people believe and act like they have power over others. They only poison their own environment and affect all who enter it. That adds nothing to any environment. Anyways, most importantly Alysia, you got your money back.

ALYSIA: How true. How true. Thanks again, Endra.

Alysia hands Endra a small basket of grape tomatoes.

ALYSIA: Here Endra, I want you to have these from my garden for all your help today.

ENDRA: Oh that's sweet. How nice! Thank you!

Endra waves and walks off to her office.

***

ACT 4

ENDRA'S OFFICE

Endra is sitting at her desk, and grabs a grape tomato, placing it in her mouth. Just then the door opens wide. Paulie walks in and approaches Endra's desk.

PAULIE: Hey, is that a grape tomato?

ENDRA: (CHEWS AND SWALLOWS) Excuse me?

PAULIE: (EXTENDING HAND) Hi. I'm Paulie Abruzzi. I'm your 2 o'clock.

ENDRA: Oh, hello. . . .

PAULIE: Would you mind if I have one?

Paulie reaches into her basket of grape tomatoes and grabs a handful. He shoves all of them into his mouth.

PAULIE: Oh, they're sweet!

ENDRA: (HORRIFIED) Maybe you should take a seat.

PAULIE: So, you're a matchmaker huh? You must know big Jimmy Hunt. Oh yeah, he was a big matchmaker back in the day. I know people who know him. And he just lost his shirt you know. Maybe that DeservingLove.com ran his business into the ground. Jimmy went to my alma mater. I went to Boston State, a great school. I hear you're pretty successful, you must have gone there too, I bet.

ENDRA: (NONCOMITTALLY) That's a strong aura of yellow with a tinge of red. Must have spleen issues.

She reaches down and presses on an acupuncture point just above her right ankle.

PAULIE: Yeah, yeah! Yellow and red! That's our colors. I'm a season ticket holder. What year did you graduate? Bet 'cha I know someone from your class. Remember that little movie theater you could sneak in the back and watch movies there for free? Yeah, I took a lot of dates there and the popcorn wasn't bad too. We always got free refills.

ENDRA: (ROLLS HER EYES) So why don't you tell me what you're looking for?

All of a sudden there is a knock on the door and a delivery woman comes in with a package.

DELIVERY WOMAN: Oh, sorry to interrupt Endra. I just have a package for you that I need you to sign for.

PAULIE: Hey, that's from the Trappistine Nuns. Their chocolates are awesome but very expensive, especially coming from nuns. Don't you think?

Endra stares at Paulie and then reaches down below her knee and presses on another acupuncture point.

DELIVERY WOMAN: Looks like someone is going to have a nice dessert for themselves tonight. (LOOKING AT ENDRA)

Endra signs the receipt and smiles.

ENDRA: Thank you.

DELIVERY WOMAN: (SMILES AT ENDRA) Ok goodbye. (SMILES AT PAULIE) Goodbye.

The delivery woman walks out.

PAULIE: Yeah, see I don't have a problem with women. I think she kind of liked me too, don't you think so Endra? (WINKS) Yeah, but you know I'm the CEO of a multi-million dollar company and I don't know how it would look to other people if I showed up with a delivery woman on my arm. So, hey you gonna open up that box of chocolates?

ENDRA: (LOOKS AT THE CHOCOLATES AND SAYS TO HERSELF) Fool me once . . . (SAYS TO PAULIE) No. This is not for you.

PAULIE: You sure? I could help you open them. They look delicious.

Endra puts the box of chocolates on the shelf behind her desk.

ENDRA: So describe to me what you want. You know, in a partner . . .

PAULIE: Well, as I was saying, I am the CEO of a multi-million dollar company. I travel all over the world. I am in charge of a lot of people. I have made a lot of people money. And I have made a lot of sacrifices. I have given lots of people jobs. Thousands of jobs. And listen, sweetheart, I know money. The Board of Directors looks up to me. My employees look up to me and I never forget: Cash is King.

ENDRA: Again, so what are you looking for in a partner?

PAULIE: I'll plug you into what I'm looking for.

Endra gets up and starts to walk around her office. She picks up dried ginger root, smells it and holds it in her hands, and then walks over to spinach and kale. Paulie follows her.

PAULIE: Hey, what's that? Can I have a taste?

ENDRA: (BREAKS OF A PIECE AND HANDS IT TO HIM) Here. That's enough.

PAULIE: Ooh, what was that? My stomach feels a little better. Forget it. Let's get back to me and finding me a date. Because you know, that's why I'm here. Okay. I want someone with a good job, someone who can take care of stuff. I want someone who is a good cook. And then I think I'd like . . . . Hey, you're not listening to me.

Endra stops and glances at Paulie.

PAULIE: I'm paying you, so don't forget, sweetheart, you work for me now.

PAULIE: (GLANCES DOWN) Hey, nice Doc Martens, those are some nice shoes Endra.

There is a second knock on the door.

ENDRA: This is unusual. Come in!

A man pokes his head in.

MAN FROM PAULIE'S OFFICE: Oh, hi, is Paulie here? We just finished our meeting and there are some left over sandwiches. We didn't see Paulie in the office and his secretary said he was here.

PAULIE: (GETS UP QUICK, GRABS A BAG AND LOOKS IN) Oh that's great, thanks. Look there's turkey, and what's that, tuna? Endra, come on help yourself.

The man leaves.

PAULIE: Yeah, they all take care of me. They are all townies, Endra. Come on Endra, have a sandwich.

ENDRA: Why don't you give me more information?

PAULIE: (WITH A MOUTH FULL OF FOOD) I want boobs. Big boobs. (CONTINUES MUNCHING) I mean it would be a real bonus if she had the best boobs ever. I'd like her to have a nice car too, a beautiful car. A car that smells good. (HE GETS UP AND WALKS AROUND) Boy that sandwich was delicious. Oh I feel so bloated. (STOPS AT HER HERBS) Hey, these smell good too. Are these edible?

ENDRA: No those herbs aren't edible. They wouldn't be good for you.

PAULIE: Oh, okay. No worries. I won't touch them.

ENDRA: What other types of women have you dated?

PAULIE: What am I doing your job now? Why am I going to tell you what I've done? Isn't it your job to find someone that I want? You're supposed to be figuring out what's right for me. You're the matchmaker.

ENDRA: (TO HERSELF) I'm not getting anywhere energetically with this guy. It's time for a change. (SHE PAUSES A MOMENT AND SAYS TO PAULIE) Alright, do you have any questions for me?

PAULIE: Fee. What is your fee? What does it include? What's involved? What kind of paperwork do I have to fill out?

Endra doesn't answer but looks at him with a blank stare.

PAULIE: You know there are some free places out there. Ever hear of Flint.com? Everything is free. All their events. Do you have any free events?

ENDRA: No.

PAULIE: How about dates? Do you cover them?

ENDRA: No.

PAULIE: You know, DeservingLove.com has free events and they even give you free pens to fill out their forms and you can keep them. That's free advertising for them.

ENDRA: You should join DeservingLove.com.

PAULIE: Oh yeah, I was going to join but I don't have to. I know someone there. If anyone worthwhile comes through, he'll just pass me her number. It's good to know people, Endra. They take care of me. And by the way, if I meet someone through you and we get divorced, do I get a refund? You know, of your fee?

Paulie's cellphone rings.

PAULIE: (AS HE STRETCHES BACK IN THE CHAIR) Oh hold on, this is really important.

Endra goes to the corner of her office.

ENDRA: (TO HERSELF) Too many issues. His stomach, his spleen, a never ending hole. He needs a mother, and that's not me.

PAULIE: (ON THE PHONE) Oh, who? Marilyn? She's hanging out with Chad? They're what? I didn't know that. How long have they been dating? (PAUSES, SURPRISED) Wow. That's news. What? Who's looking for me? I don't like that. If he says he needs me, I want nothing to do with him. That's pencils down for me. And reply to that email. Tell the investors the budget is almost done for the year. I know it's June but they love me.

Endra walks over to Paulie and taps on her watch.

ENDRA: Time.

PAULIE: (WINKS AND WHISPERS TO ENDRA) Hey, I might have more clients for you. (INTO PHONE) I gotta go.

Paulie hangs up and stands.

PAULIE: Hey, what if you and I go out and grab a coffee? (LAUGHS) I guess then I wouldn't have a fee to pay, right? (LAUGHS) Do you know anyone around here who could give us a good deal on coffee?

ENDRA: (SHAKING HER HEAD) No.

PAULIE: Oh wait, I just remembered. Pepino's is right around the corner. And they have the best raviolis. We could split them! If we leave now we can probably still catch the lunch menu, and save a few bucks.

Paulie touches his chest and pulls a bag of nuts from his top pocket and begins to eat them.

PAULIE: Hey Endra, if you play your cards right sweetheart . . . you know I'm not a six figure salary guy, I'm a seven figure guy.

Paulie walks over to the window.

PAULIE: You see those multi-million dollar homes over there? One of them is mine. It's a nice neighborhood. Everyone's pretty much into the community, except for one guy. He avoids me but he's an ass.

ENDRA: Paulie, time's up.

PAULIE: (RAISES AND LOWERS HIS EYEBROWS IN UNISON) I'm quite a catch Endra. Huh? Maybe that will save me on your fee. Huh? Huh? (PUTS HIS ELBOW OUT TO HER AND TAPS HER)

Suddenly the door flies open.

ENDRA: (TO HERSELF) Knight. Ahh, as always your timing is impeccable.

PAULIE: (TURNS AROUND) Oh, is this your next client?

ENDRA: (LAUGHS) Client? No.

Paulie winks at Endra and heads for the open door. As he gets up and walks, he stubs his toe.

PAULIE: Ouch! I stubbed my big toe. (REACHES DOWN TO HIS TOE) Hmm, I feel bloated again. I'm gonna head out now, Endra. If you find anyone give me a call, send her my way.

ENDRA: Well, when the time is right, I certainly will.

Paulie limps out.

***

ACT 5

ENDRA'S COTTAGE

Knight and Endra are walking through the garden, picking some vegetables and pulling out some weeds. Knight stops and looks at Endra.

KNIGHT: So, mi inamorata, about my impeccable timing . .

ENDRA: Yes, with you, timing is impeccable. Perfect in fact. The energy created an abundance of interactions today.

KNIGHT: As energy does.

ENDRA: It was give and take all day. It reminded me that when energy in your environment reaches an extreme, it must rebalance itself. Much like the Pirate Ship ride at an amusement park when it hits its peak and it must rebalance itself and swing in the opposite direction.

KNIGHT: Yes, left to its own devices, energy will rebalance itself.

ENDRA: Yet others often intervene before things balance again because they are frustrated with waiting. When in actuality, waiting is the servant to time. And waiting creates all sorts of pain.

KNIGHT: Yes my dear. Thinking and hoping for the pain to decrease or the time to shorten doesn't help. Pain can only be taken away by the one who is creating and holding onto it.

ENDRA: And intervening doesn't help. I only do what the energy asks of me.

KNIGHT: What more would there be to do, my love?

ENDRA: Nothing more. Such as today, the nun reached an extreme when her untruths peaked loudly and then rebalanced, bringing her to silence. At Maxmart the energy assisted me in getting in and out of a tough situation, quickly. The employee was going to hold onto her pain and allow it to ruin her environment and anyone that came into that environment.

KNIGHT: And with no wait, there is no frustration, and no pain, because there is no time. With that last client of yours, you planted the seed and nurtured the energy beyond what was expected.

ENDRA: Yes, so much stagnant spleen energy with Paulie. Being in that space is always difficult.

KNIGHT: And intervening would only have caused you to be trapped in the pain.

ENDRA: Right. His pain would have become clogged, causing me to wait . . .

KNIGHT: (LAUGHS) Not you though. Time is on your side.

ENDRA: (LAUGHS) Yes. It is quite challenging staying out of the time trap when everyone around you is obsessed with time. Living amongst these people, it's hard not to fall into bad habits, every now and then. So I reminded myself that time was up.

KNIGHT: Time was up. And time was out, and away from you. Where others go with it is their business, not ours.

ENDRA: Agreed. I respond and interact only with the energy, always enhancing balance.

KNIGHT: And thus the energy responds as well, working with and for you, quite brilliantly.

ENDRA: (PLAYFULLY LAUGHS) I love communicating with the energy. The problem and the drama go away and the solution rises to the top.

KNIGHT: Acting from the solution is much more powerful.

ENDRA: And the solution presents itself with perfect timing.

KNIGHT: So, now I ask you, mi inamorata, was my timing impeccable even without my intervening?

ENDRA: Ahh my darling, yes. I can work with time pretty well on my own. (LEANS IN TOWARDS KNIGHT) Although, I would never refuse any offer from you . . .

KNIGHT: (LAUGHS) By the way, those grape tomatoes over there look ripe.

ENDRA: (LAUGHS) Thank you for coming to *save me* but the energy was already fully surrounding me.

KNIGHT: But I wanted to surround you too.

Knight comes from behind Endra and wraps his arms around her.

ENDRA: You know Knight, I've been using acupressure points all day to direct the energy, to move. And so my dear, do you catch any movement from this one?

Endra rubs a point on her ear.

KNIGHT: Hmm.

ENDRA: How about this one?

Endra rubs a point below her navel.

KNIGHT: Oh yes, that one I know.

ENDRA: This?

Endra rubs a point on the inside of her knee.

KNIGHT: (WITH EYES ABLAZE) I know exactly what that point is for.

Knight turns Endra to face him, pulls her into his arms and gives her a kiss. He grabs her hand and together they walk back to the cottage.

***

ACT 6

THE BLUE BOOK OF ENERGY

On the table in the hallway of Endra's cottage, Endra's blue book of energy opens. The book settles upon page one hundred and twenty. The following invocation pulses as candlelight flickers on the words around it:

"My environment is self-sufficient and expresses itself with consistency allowing abundance and direction."

***

THE END

Endra: Anecdotes of a Modern Day Witch

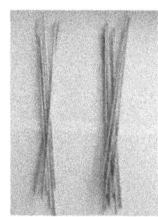

Phase 5: Cha Ching, Here's Your Change

by Polonious

ENDRA: ANECDOTES OF A MODERN DAY WITCH

Phase 5 – Cha Ching, Here's Your Change

<u>CAST OF CHARACTERS (in order of appearance):</u>

ENDRA..........................*Energy maven living in Windover.*
JONATHAN ....*Works in Endra's office building,*
                               an Attorney
WOMAN 1.....................*Tenant in Endra's office building*
WOMAN 2.....................*Tenant in Endra's office building*
WOMAN 3.....................*Tenant in Endra's office building*
MAN 1 ....*Tenant in Endra's office building*
RANDOM MALE VOICE *Random Male Voice*
ALYSIA ....*Works in Endra's office building,*
                               fashion designer
TENANT 1.....................*Tenant in Endra's office building*
TENANT 2.....................*Tenant in Endra's office building*
TONY ....*Maintenance/Repairman in*
                               Endra's building
MIA...............................*Endra's Client*
ROBERT RELINKSION *Owner of Endra's office building*
MRS. RELINKSION ....*Wife of Robert Relinksion*
MS. RELINKSION.......*Daughter of Robert Relinksion*
PRESS AGENT 1 ....*Press agent at Press Conference*
PRESS AGENT 2 ....*Press agent at Press Conference*
PRESS AGENT 3 ....*Press agent at Press Conference*
KNIGHT ....*Endra's companion and lover*
EXTRAS........................*Various tenants milling around in*
   building, chanting and getting rowdy. Many random voices
   in the building and on the street. Crowds at Press
   Conference. People with cameras and microphones at
   Press Conference. Random crowds.

SETTINGS IN WINDOVER:

♦*Endra's Office building*   ♦*Endra's Office*
♦*Street outside Endra's office*   ♦*Endra's Garden*
♦*Endra's Cottage*

Phase 5: Cha Ching, Here's Your Change

ACT 1

ENDRA ARRIVES AT HER OFFICE BUILDING

There is a mob of angry people inside and outside of Endra's office building. The people inside congregate around Jonathan, an attorney who rents in the same building as Endra.

ENDRA: (WAVES TO JONATHAN) Jonathan?

JONATHAN: (NODS) I . . .

WOMAN 1: What are we going to do?

WOMAN 2: I can't believe this. Can they really get away with this?

ENDRA: Jonathan, what's going on here?

WOMAN 3: (TO ENDRA, INTERRUPTING) Well Relinksion, you know, your landlord, is going up on all of our rents, *including yours*. When you get to your office you will see your notice. I know how to handle this! We need to march!

ENDRA: Jonathan, when you get a moment?

JONATHAN: (TO ENDRA) Please . . .

WOMAN 1: We need to get signs together.

MAN 1: Yeah! We should come up with some slogans.

RANDOM MALE VOICE: (YELLS) How about this one? "You-stink. Re-link!"

JONATHAN: (ROLLS HIS EYES) That's not going to get us anywhere.

Endra continues to her office. She grabs a note taped to her door and goes into her office. Outside a mob is growing in the hallway. They are embroiled in heated conversations.

***

ACT 2

ENDRA'S OFFICE

SCENE 1: ENDRA READING THE NOTICE

ENDRA: (READING) Effective immediately . . . This is what's going to happen . . . Your rates . . .

Jonathan pops his head into Endra's office. In the background are lots of noises and yelling. The squeaks and smells of markers are in the air.

JONATHAN: Endra . . .

ENDRA: Jonathan, come in here and get away from all that. What is this about?

JONATHAN: I've done some research but the people here are just clueless. They don't understand. But what I found out is that Relinksion owns all the street lights in our town.

ENDRA: They own the streetlights? What's that got to do with anything?

JONATHAN: I know, I know. Let me explain. There was a deal Relinksion made with the town years ago. Relinksion donates the filament that keeps the lights burning bright.

ENDRA: (TO HERSELF) So they have control over what people see . . .

JONATHAN: In return Relinksion holds the title to the property. The property being the streetlights.

ENDRA: (TO JONATHAN) And that ties to this how?

JONATHAN: Relinksion now wants to upgrade and repair their lights. To do this they want to hold a community fundraiser to pay for it. However for them to fund the fundraiser they need money.

ENDRA: So they need money. To fund, their fundraiser.

JONATHAN: Yes. By raising our rent, Relinksion is hoping the additional net proceeds will pay for their fundraiser. Which in turn will hopefully raise enough money to fix the lights.

ENDRA: What a convoluted mess.

JONATHAN: I know and they are doing this with all the buildings they own in town. And you know, they own almost all of them.

ENDRA: (ROLLS HER EYES) Usually a fundraiser is funded by volunteers and donated items and services.

JONATHAN: I agree and this is ridiculous. Relinksion has no volunteers or goods of their own to donate. And so they are raising our rent for funds. That's how they are posturing it.

Alysia, out of breath, opens Endra's door, enters and shuts it quickly behind her.

ALYSIA: Geez, I just got in from a long weekend and three women bombarded me and asked me to make t-shirts. For some cause? Or some march that they planned?

ENDRA: A march? Don't mind about them. Jonathan and I are discussing it now.

ALYSIA: So Jonathan, is our rent going up?

JONATHAN: Yes, that's our donation to the cause.

ALYSIA: (CONFUSED) Cause? Do you mean charity? Are we talking about a charity? I mean what charity are we talking about here?

ENDRA: Jonathan, let me see if I can explain it. So, Relinksion is increasing our rent so they can contribute to a fundraiser that will upgrade the lights that they already own because they donate the filament that is also paid for by our rent. Did I get that right Jonathan?

JONATHAN: Yup. Yes you did.

The three continue to hear bangs outside and stomps on the floor.

VOICES FROM THE CROWD OUTSIDE:
(SHOUTING) Reee-think . . . Reee-link. Reee-think . . . Reee-link.

Endra, Alysia and Jonathan look at each other.

ALYSIA: I'm still confused.

JONATHAN: Well basically they have increased our rent and legally it appears binding.

ENDRA: Well let's hold on. Let's not jump into their story yet.

Chants grow louder outside.

VOICES FROM THE CROWD OUTSIDE:
(SHOUTING) Reee-think . . . Reee-link. Reee-think . . . Reee-link.

JONATHAN: Oh I better get back out there.

Jonathan turns around, opens the door and walks out. A man's voice yells out from the hallway.

MAN 1: (YELLS) Jonathan, come over here and check out what we've done!

VOICES FROM THE CROWD OUTSIDE:
(SHOUTING) Reee-think . . . Reee-link. Youu-stink . . . Reee-link.

WOMAN 2: We need to choose one and stick with it . . . (VOICE TRAILS OFF)

Alysia quickly closes the door behind Jonathan.

ALYSIA: You know, Endra, I don't mind contributing to the community, but something about this feels wrong.

ENDRA: It feels wrong because it's being called charity yet there is nothing charitable about it. We'll keep in touch dear. Focus on your upcoming fashion show.

Alysia opens the door to leave Endra's office. The chanting outside has gained momentum.

VOICES FROM THE CROWD OUTSIDE:
 (SHOUTING) Reee-think . . . Reee-link.

Alysia looks back at Endra and smiles.

ALYSIA: (SMIRKING) I . . . need . . . a . . . drink.

They both laugh as she leaves. Meanwhile, a mob is now outside in the hallway holding signs and chanting, walking up and down the hallway and the street outside.

SCENE 2: NATURE'S CONJURING

Endra walks to her window, opens it. Endra closes her eyes, puts her hands on her chest and releases a big sigh. She looks out towards the trees.

ENDRA: I-Ching, I feel the energy changing. You remind us that everything is meaningful and temporary in an interconnected Universe.

 Endra can't help but notice the huge mobs of people now gathering out around the trees, street and building. The skies get dark and there is a burst of rain.

ENDRA: Ahh, rain. Like tears you flow, moving the stagnant chi. What is stuck and frustrated should now break up and disperse into pieces, and clear the pent up energy below.

 Endra looks down and realizes that the mob has not moved despite the rain. Their chants have only gotten louder. The trees start blowing ferociously and the wind is howling.

 Endra steps away from the window and reaches over to her set of yarrow sticks on the side of her counter. She picks them up and holds them close to her chest as she closes her eyes and chants.

ENDRA: Beautiful yarrow sticks of the I-Ching. Feel my energy and my intent as I embrace your guidance. I start with the 64 divine hexagrams allowing them to filter to the two, yin and yang. As opposites they flow together ever twisting and turning, reminding us everything changes.

Endra looks out to the trees swaying in the strong winds. Amid the turmoil she makes out two images formed within the branches of the trees. She interprets the images surrounding the interpersonal patterns of change. She recreates the two hexagrams with her yarrow sticks, drawing the following:

ENDRA: <u>Lesser Yin over Yang.</u> The Middle Daughter. Fire. Yin is squashed by an abundance of creativity, passion and a desire for notoriety. With you, spring turns towards summer. <u>And Lesser Yang over Yin.</u> The Middle Son. A flowing river. Yang is overpowered by emotions and relationships. Yet with both of you young immature forces, there is pure balance.

Endra looks outside once more.

ENDRA: Wind naked to the eye,
you squeal, you howl, you blow.
A blade of grass sways back and forth
to your ever-changing flow.
A mighty ship sails fast and far
with your charging power.
Yet topples in the wildest of waves,
during your storm's worst hour.

She turns to the window.

ENDRA: Which wind will prevail today?
Nature be our guide right now,
as chaos marks our place.
Bring a subtle balance back,
as we reclaim our space.

*Endra looks once again out the window. She connects
deeper with the yarrow sticks as she turns her head to
listen to the wind. In response, she recreates one last
hexagram with her yarrow sticks:*

ENDRA: <u>Wiser and Greater Yang</u>. Full summer, heat and
heaven. This most powerful and wise, extreme of yang
comes to penetrate this space. With yin absent, things can
run amok.

*Endra inhales with determination, knowing the full power
of wiser and greater yang without its opposite, greater
yin, to soften its mighty blow. Holding her yarrow sticks
close to her chest, she recites:*

ENDRA: Earth ground our feet below,
and air let good thoughts fly.
Water bend, and break the flow,
and wood neutralize
all pain from the sky.

*Outside there is one big gust of wind that knocks over one
tree in the distance, away from the mob of people. Four
power lines topple over with it. The storm ends. Endra
hearing the loud sound outside, immediately grabs her
yarrow sticks and gently places them on her counter.*

Endra closes her window and moves back into her office and notices the lights are out.

The crowd within the office hallway is now yelling about the lights being off and the elevator out of order. Alysia opens Endra's door and speaks from the threshold.

ALYSIA: Hey, Endra are you okay in there? The power is off everywhere.

ENDRA: Yes. I'm fine.

Tenants gather in the hallway.

TENANT 1: Wow. This is crazy. The lines are down. There is no power.

TENANT 2: Is anyone stuck in the elevator? Does anyone know what happened?

Into Endra's office walks Tony, the Building Maintenance Manager, with tools, tape measure, etc.

ENDRA: Hey, Anthony, how are you? I haven't seen you in a while.

TONY: Yeah! A buddy and I went up north for a few days to have a few beers.

Tony leans into Endra and laughs.

TONY: Figured we'd go and see the foliage, except the damn trees kept getting in the way.

ENDRA: (SMILES AND LOOKS AT HIM) That's a clever one.

TONY: Yeah, we made a mistake in our route and ended up coming back earlier than we thought.

ENDRA: Oh that's too bad. You had to cut your vacation short.

TONY: Yeah, I went with Rocky, my old police partner. Geez, every time we go he says he'll take care of the directions. Every time he gets us lost. I say, "Rocky, most people make hundreds of mistakes, you make the same mistake a hundred times." (LAUGHS HYSTERICALLY)

Alysia laughs.

ENDRA: (SMILES) That's funny. But there's some truth in that too.

ALYSIA: Tony, that's really funny. You must have a wall of quotes somewhere. But on a serious note, do you know what's going on here?

TONY: Yeah, I'll tell ya. We're not going to have any power for the rest of the day. That tree took down four power lines. It's going to take the electric company at least a solid 24 hours if not more to get everything up and running again. So you should all just pack up and head down to Scratch O'Reilly's and grab a beer. Tell Ted I sent ya. He owns the place. He'll take care of ya.

Tony points to the hall, towards the other tenants.

TONY: But don't bring those dopes. (YELLS DOWN THE HALLWAY) Everyone go home. There is no power. (WAVES HIS HANDS) No power.

Alysia and Tony head down the hallway.

ALYSIA: Ugh. Of all days, *today*. Today I'm having fabric measured and cut. I'm going to have to reschedule.

TONY: Geez I don't know what to tell you Alysia. You don't want to be hanging out in this building without any power, especially to measure and cut. (POINTS AT ALYSIA) You know Alysia, if you have to cut that expensive fabric, remember: measure twice, and cut just once.

Endra locks her door and leaves the building.

***

ACT 3

NEXT DAY, ENDRA'S OFFICE

SCENE 1: MIA

The power is on. There is a knock on Endra's door. Mia enters her doorway.

ENDRA: You must be Mia. Come in and sit down. How can I help you?

MIA: Oh, no I don't need any help. I'm just here to find my soulmate. (LEANS IN AND SAYS) By the way, did you know that there are protests going on downstairs? That's where I got this comical t-shirt.

ENDRA: (LOOKS AT MIA'S SHIRT AND READS) Ree . . . think, Ree . . . link?

MIA: Yeah, it's a funny shirt but the money goes to a good charity and that's why I bought it. Oh and I brought you a pineapple.

ENDRA: Oh, a pineapple . . . Okay. (PUTS IT ON THE SIDE OF HER DESK)

MIA: The pineapple is a sign of welcome. I'm welcoming you into my light. I'm a healer. I take care of all my patients. I love them, and they love me back.

ENDRA: (IN DISBELIEF) Really?

MIA: My shaman, Jedidiah, holds seminars for thousands of people and Jedidiah teaches us that we should all give and give and that's what I do. And in return I only ask for my patients to be happy. Jedidiah's really good, Endra. I'd love for you to meet him. Jedidiah says that when God gives you a gift, it is meant to be shared.

ENDRA: Why don't we just focus on the soulmate, today?

MIA: Okay. Umm, I like to cook. I don't mind cleaning. And I work very hard. I like to make other people happy and comfortable. (SIGHS) You know, I just like to be happy. And I love animals.

ENDRA: And you want . . .

MIA: Someone to enjoy all of this with.

ENDRA: Enjoying all of what with you?

MIA: Following God's path with me. I don't want anything else. I don't need anything else. If I can give help to others, and to my soulmate, of course, then I have done my job.

ENDRA: So you don't want anything, in return. You just want to give.

MIA: Oh that's such a beautiful way of putting it.

ENDRA: And you're saying that you give everything to your patients and ask for nothing in return. Is this true?

MIA: Yes. That's the God's honest truth.

ENDRA: Do you at least receive some form of payment?

MIA: Yes I receive some payment. But you and I both know it's not about money. It's about the healing energy I give.

ENDRA: Okay. If you give healing energy, how do you replenish this healing energy?

MIA: Nah, I don't need to recharge.

ENDRA: Well, if you don't have a balance, you deplete yourself.

MIA: Oh that's sweet of you to think of me like that. But I'm okay, really.

ENDRA: If you don't replenish for yourself, you must be taking from someone else.

MIA: I don't do that. I heal people.

ENDRA: If you give to others from an empty pot, you are taking from someone else's pot to replenish your own pot.

MIA: Wait. I would never do that. I'm a good person. I do lots of charity work.

ENDRA: And what you are giving away as charity was never yours to give.

MIA: I'm not so sure I understand.

ENDRA: Maybe you should re-think what you believe.

MIA: Ohhh.

ENDRA: True charity is giving from a space of abundance. It never takes from another person. Anything other than that is not charity.

MIA: Ohhh. I never thought of it like that. I'm late for my next patient. Maybe I should come back, if I can find the time in between my patients.

ENDRA: And, you might want to re-think the shirt you are wearing.

MIA: Oh? This shirt was just a donation to a charity. It's just a limerick.

ENDRA: Limerick? Oh no, it is a slant on Mr. Relinksion.

MIA: Ohh. You mean Mr. Robert Relinksion? Oh my God, that's my next patient. I can't wear this shirt. He is supposed to come in after some speech today. He's such a nice guy. Did you know he donates a 100 percent of his income to charity?

ENDRA: (TO HERSELF) Hmm, a speech?

Mia leaves. Endra gets up, takes a deep breath, goes to the window, and sees a growing crowd of people outside, and a podium. Many of the people are wearing shirts that say "Re-think Re-link."

SCENE 2: ON THE STREET OUTSIDE
OF ENDRA'S OFFICE BUILDING

Robert Relinksion is giving a press conference to the crowd to address concerns. The media is there. Endra has a bird's eye view as she is watching from her window above.

Sitting behind Robert are two women. One is his wife, smiling, always at the cameras. There is a duffle bag by her feet. The other is his daughter, sitting next to her mother crocheting.

Robert Relinksion approaches the podium. Part of the crowd is booing, part softly chanting "Re-think, Re-link."

ROBERT: (TAPPING ON THE MICROPHONE) Okay, settle down. You guys have been heard. Now be quiet. Be quiet now.

The crowd starts to quiet down.

ROBERT: I came out here today for the community. I know everybody is upset about costs but this community is worth having these lights fixed. The safety of the women and children in this town is of our utmost importance. (MOTIONS TO HIS WIFE AND DAUGHTER WHO GIGGLE) And we will come together as a community to ensure the safety of all.

PRESS AGENT 1: These demonstrators are here protesting. What are you going to do for them?

ROBERT: Do for them? We are trying to do for everyone. And you press need to get this story straight.

PRESS AGENT 1: But what are you going to do to resolve this?

ROBERT: (POINTING TO THE CROWD) Well first of all these protestors didn't get a permit. So they are already here illegally. But we are going to move beyond that to the bigger issue.

ENDRA: (TO HERSELF) Here comes a wind storm of another kind.

Chants of "Re-think, Re-link" are growing in the crowd.

Robert's wife looks nervously into the crowd, reaches into her duffle bag and takes out a new pair of heels and starts changing her shoes.

ROBERT: (HOLDING UP HIS HAND) Excuse me! Excuse me! Listen. For those of you who are not interested in helping this community, we don't want you here. Chant elsewhere. I came out to talk to you and address this important issue in our community. Relinksion started out with nothing. But we built these buildings to help these entrepreneurs (MOTIONING TO THE CROWD) and worked really hard with this community. We have created thousands of jobs and we have supported each other all along the way. And now it's time we support our families and our friends. It's time to extend the charity. We've been very successful and believe in giving back.

The crowd quiets down.

ROBERT: We have had an extensive charitable history and dammit we are not abandoning it now.

ENDRA: (QUIETYLY) Charity? What a false definition for charity.

PRESS AGENT 2: Can you expand upon this charity work?

ROBERT: Now that's a great question. We have huge programs in place. A lot of our charity has gone unnoticed because it's been more individualized. But now we're bringing it to the community. (PUTS HIS HAND OUT) Don't we all want to help the community?

The chants diminish. The crowd erupts in cheers. Robert's wife smiles in the cameras and reaches down to change her shoes again. This time it's a pair of chic boots.

ROBERT: Just like the signs in our buildings will tell you. We give and give to local charities. 100 percent of our net proceeds. Yes 100 percent!

VOICES IN THE CROWD: (MURMURING AND GROWING) 100 percent, who knew?

MORE VOICES IN THE CROWD: (MURMURING AND GROWING) I didn't know 100 percent, did you?

Crowd murmurs continue.

PRESS AGENT 2: 100 percent, wow, that's impressive.

ROBERT: And you media better make sure you get these numbers correct. Those are the facts.

PRESS AGENT 3: But wait a second, you said 100 percent of the net proceeds. Can you define "net" for us? Net of what?

ROBERT: You're just getting caught up in technical mumbo jumbo here. Defining words doesn't solve problems. The important issue here is the charity. And getting these lights fixed for the safety of our community.

VOICES IN THE CROWD: (MURMURING AND GROWING) That's right. It's about the charity.

MORE VOICES IN THE CROWD: (MURMURING AND GROWING) And safety? Don't you care about people?

ROBERT: Okay. That's all the time I have right now. I have an important meeting. But rest assured, I will make sure that this community gets what it needs.

ENDRA: (TO HERSELF) What it needs or what you need?

Crowd cheers and disbands. Endra shuts her window, grabs the I-Ching sticks from the counter and places them in her coat. She closes her office and heads home.

***

ACT 4

OUTSIDE ENDRA'S COTTAGE

Endra and Knight are exiting her cottage. Endra carries her yarrow, I-Ching sticks.

ENDRA: Let's go for a walk Knight.

KNIGHT: Let's darling.

> *They stroll into the forest of pine trees behind her cottage to where there is a grove of trees and desert sand. In the middle of the sand is an Elephant Tree which is highlighted by the moon.*

ENDRA: Our walk has taken us to the Elephant Tree.

KNIGHT: (LAUGHS) And is that a surprise?

ENDRA: This Elephant Tree is our elephant in the room. (LAUGHS TOO) Everyone has an elephant in the room.

KNIGHT: So true, my dear.

ENDRA: Some avoid the elephant, some hide from it, and some continuously feed it. Yet the elephant left to its own accord takes care of itself.

KNIGHT: Yes, my dear, but you are forgetting one thing. It's honoring and trusting the energy of the elephant that allows one to do that. You have forgotten that you do that so well. Not everyone has that awareness.

ENDRA: Yes, that's true. I prefer not to get embroiled in the story or events. (MOTIONING TO THE BRANCHES) I just let the elephant be.

KNIGHT: How wise. Getting intertwined either confuses or distracts the energy, or slows the energy's processing down.

ENDRA: Not getting ensnared allows the elements to come together in a more powerful and natural way. The I-Ching sticks expressed this to me in a very powerful way today.

KNIGHT: Mi inamorata, please do what you came her to do.

Endra walks closer to the Elephant Tree, takes the I-Ching sticks from her coat and holds them close to her chest.

ENDRA: I return you wood to your place beside the elements. May you root and recharge and undo any memories hindered by mankind's beliefs.

Endra places the sticks under the tree.

ENDRA: Thank you for clearly defining the truth. In doing this you have balanced the energy of nature as well as my own space.

It starts to rain.

KNIGHT: A perfect gift for the rain.

Knight grabs Endra's hand and they walk back to the cottage.

***

ACT 5

THE NEXT DAY

Endra gets to her office building and there is a notice taped on the outside door. She reads.

ENDRA: Due to unforeseen circumstances Relinksion is going to have to cancel the fundraiser and forego any charitable distributions. To that end, Relinksion will not be increasing your rent. Relinksion will, however, find the ways and means to continue our charitable efforts.

Endra smiles, and opens the door and walks in the building. In the hallway she meets Alysia.

ALYSIA: (LAUGHING) Hey, Endra! I see you read the one notice.

ENDRA: Yes. Interesting turn of events.

ALYSIA: Relinksion isn't making their charitable donation. Something else must be up.

ENDRA: It seems so.

Jonathan enters the building.

ALYSIA: Good morning Jonathan. Do you know what happened?

JONATHAN: Oh, you mean the notice? There's so much to talk about here.

ALYSIA: Yeah. Tell me about it. Yes the notice.

JONATHAN: The notice is our official written notification that our rents are no longer going to be increased. Relinksion however is also not going to be able to make their donation to the community.

ALYSIA: Well either way that's good news to me.

Tony comes out of the elevator and joins the conversation. He walks up with a smile.

ALYSIA: (POINTING) Tony, what's with the shirt?

TONY: What? (LAUGHING) Isn't this the shirt everyone's wearing?

Tony is wearing one of the "Re-think Re-link" shirts. In black marker the "Re-think" has a line through it. Handwritten above it is "You stink."

ENDRA: (LAUGHS) That's creative.

ALYSIA: (READING AND LAUGHING) "You stink" Re-link?!

TONY: Yeah, I found a crate of them out back. I left one in everyone's office. But I made this little change to mine.

Endra, Jonathan, and Alysia laugh.

JONATHAN: Well, the story is over now, Tony. Because due to unforeseen circumstances, they are not raising our rent.

TONY: I'll give you unforeseen circumstances. Let me tell you a little story about Mr. Jeffrey Long Pockets. You know, Mr. Relinksion.

JONATHAN: Tony, isn't the correct term Johnny Long Pockets?

TONY: Jonathan, for your sake, let's call him Jeffrey Long Pockets. His pockets are really long until you come to those Jeffrey shoes that his wife likes.

ALYSIA: Jeffrey Long Pockets. That's so funny! I love that. I'm gonna call him that from now on. To tell you the truth though, I do love those shoes.

TONY: Never mind that. So, you want to know the real truth?

ENDRA: Of course we want the truth, Anthony.

ALYSIA: He couldn't keep it from us anyways. Spill it Tony. What's the scoop?

TONY: Well I was talking with Gerry Klipper. He works at the loading docks over at Relinksion's home office. He and I go way back.

JONATHAN: You know everybody Tony.

TONY: (LAUGHS) Ha Ha. Yeah, I know Jonathan. So I guess, the legal, mailing, even paper expenses got to be too much, even for Relinksion.

ALYSIA: Paper expenses? Are you kidding me?

TONY: Yeah, paper expenses. Who would have thought? All these were related to the rent increase scam and would never be covered by the new rent let alone any donation. So they scrapped it all.

ENDRA: So the cost of the paper was too much to increase our rent, to hold the fundraiser, and make any donation. Who would have thought? All this because of trees?

ALYSIA: So no donation?

JONATHAN: It looks like it isn't happening this time, my friend.

ENDRA: (SMILING) Well, on that happy note, I might just go home and celebrate. It's been a long windy week. Goodbye all.

Endra heads home.

***

ACT 6

THE BLUE BOOK OF ENERGY

Back inside Endra's cottage, the wind blows as Knight closes the bedroom door. In the hallway, a stick rolls off the bookshelf onto the table landing upon Endra's blue book of energy, as it opens in the wind. The book settles upon page sixty-eight. The following invocation pulses as candlelight flickers on the words around it:

"I honor my currency and definition of exchange, and thus, others honor it."

***

THE END

Endra:
Anecdotes
of a Modern Day
Witch

by Polonious

Phase 6:
Mirror, Mirror
on the Wall,
Who's the Bestest
of Them All?

ENDRA: ANECDOTES OF A MODERN DAY WITCH

Phase 6 – Mirror, Mirror on the Wall,
Who's the Bestest of Them All?

CAST OF CHARACTERS (in order of appearance):

HENRY ....*Owner of Henry's Flower Shop*
ENDRA........*Energy maven living in Windover.*
AL ....*Endra's client*
THULA ....*Student of Endra's, cousin to Athena*
ATHENA .....*Student of Endra's, cousin to Thula*
TIM ....*Student of Endra's*
JESSICA ......*Young girl, works at The Dark Cauldron*
ALISSA........*Follower of Locke, calls herself a witch*
MAGGIE......*Follower of Locke, calls herself a witch*
LOCKE ....*aka Chester, considers himself a head warlock*
JANE............*Follower of Locke, calls herself a witch*
BILL.............*Follower of Locke, believes himself a warlock*
KATRINA....*Follower of Locke, calls herself a witch*
CHUCK........*Endra's client*
ALLISON ....*Endra's client*
DONALD.....*Endra's client*
RITA ....*Hairdresser at Rita's Blowout Bar,*
.................*down the hall from Endra's office*
BARISTA ....*Coffee Barista at Captain Coffee Shop*
KNIGHT ......*Endra's companion and lover*
EXTRAS ......*Attendees of the dinner party in Endra's*
            garden.

SETTINGS IN WINDOVER:

♦*Henry's Flower Shop*   ♦*Henry's Greenhouse*
♦*Endra's Office*   ♦*Hallway outside Endra's Office*
♦*Captain Coffee Shop*   ♦*Endra's Cottage*

Phase 6: Mirror, Mirror on the Wall, Who's the Bestest of Them All?

ACT 1

HENRY'S FLOWER SHOP, SUNDAY AFTERNOON

SCENE 1: ENDRA ENTERS THE FLOWER SHOP

HENRY: Endra!

ENDRA: Hi Henry!

HENRY: It's great to see you!

ENDRA: And you, dear! Ahh the energy here is wonderful! I could stay here all day! Thank you again for offering to host my class.

Al potting on his knees, pokes his head out from behind a bush.

AL: Oh Endra, anytime we can help you, anytime. Because you know, Henry and I absolutely love you.

HENRY: And love what you did for us.

ENDRA: What I did? You did it for yourselves. Well, I suppose I should go and get set up. I'm going into the back, in the greenhouse?

HENRY: Yes, yes. There are already some characters back there. Do you want us to stay with you Endra, because we don't mind?

ENDRA: Oh no, thank you. You two go off and enjoy your day. Don't worry about little old me. I'm good.

AL: Okay, if you're sure. We are going to the marketplace. We love strolling through every Sunday afternoon. That's our day together.

ENDRA: Make sure you hit the shop at the very end. See Ben. That's where I love to get my special fabric.

HENRY AND AL: (TOGETHER) Ben?? (RAISING EYEBROWS)

ENDRA: Oh you two!

AL: (LAUGHING) We love you Endra. Are you sure there is nothing we can help you with?

ENDRA: Don't worry about me. I'm all set boys!

HENRY: Alright then. Make sure you just shut the lights and lock the door behind you!

ENDRA: Will do. Ta-Ta!

Henry grabs Al's arm and they walk out the door.

SCENE 2: HENRY'S GREENHOUSE

Endra enters the greenhouse. Attendees are sitting and talking amongst themselves.

ENDRA: (COUNTING WITH FINGER) 10. Hmm, that's odd. Something's off.

Endra walks in, puts her bag down at the table, takes out her papers and looks around the greenhouse taking in the attendees. She strategically moves plants around as others talk in the room. Endra approaches two women who light up and stand as she reaches them.

ENDRA: Good afternoon Thula, Athena. How are you?

THULA: Oh Endra. It's so good to see you. How are you?

ATHENA: Oh Endra. We just reread your three energy books again and we just can't get enough of them. Can we help you with that?

Endra places a plant by them.

ENDRA: Thank you. I'm all set. Just quickly rearranging some plants . . . and some pine here.

TIM: Hello.

Tim looks up at Endra and back at his notebook. Endra looks down at Tim over her glasses.

ENDRA: Hello.

Endra moves to the next attendee, lighting patchouli incense, smiling as she sees the young girl, Jessica, from "The Dark Cauldron," the local new age store.

ENDRA: Oh. Welcome. How is your schooling going?

JESSICA: Hi. Great, I'm almost done. I should have my license in another six months. I thought by taking your class I would be able to say I am certified in your energy too. We do get certificates afterwards, right?

ENDRA: Whatever you need.

Endra moves towards a group of six. She stands up straighter and looks at each one. A hearty conversation is going on between them.

ALISSA: So, you guys, I gave the most amazing reading last weekend.

MAGGIE: Hey, wait a minute, we are not supposed to discuss readings, it's not allowed. Oh, I guess you didn't take that Witchcraft class that explains why.

LOCKE: Oh, I took that. (TO ALISSA) Hey, I could give you a private lesson if you want.

ALISSA: (LOOKS AT HIM FEARFULLY AND CONTINUES) Well, maybe. But let me tell you about the reading. I had the woman's husband show up, and he's been dead for three months.

JANE: Oh, that's Mediumship. I don't want to hear about that. That's not supposed to happen in a reading. (TURNING TO LOCKE) So Locke, what have you been up to?

BILL: Oh, I got some new Tarot cards. If you want to come over I can show them to you later.

LOCKE: Hey, let's not get out of hand.

BILL: Oh, sorry Locke. I didn't think that . . . You know . . . I just thought that . . .

LOCKE: Wait a minute. Which one of you took that last Witchcraft class? Because I'm a Level Four Warlock here. And I can tell you anything you need to know.

KATRINA: Oh, that's right Locke. You know everything.

LOCKE: That's right. Don't forget I'm a High Priest Warlock. Or you'll regret it. Locke the High Priest.

JESSICA: (LOOKS OVER WITH FEAR AND MUMBLES) Oh my . . .

Endra places three cactus plants around the group of six.

ENDRA: Oh, what is your name, again? I don't remember that on my list.

Endra walks to the table with her papers and looking at the list, she places a sunflower by her desk.

LOCKE: Locke.

ENDRA: Really? I don't have that name registered for my class. Did you sign up?

LOCKE: (TO KATRINA) Hey, you told me I was all set. What did you do?

Katrina looks nervously from Locke to Endra. Endra looks over her list and smiles.

ENDRA: Oh wait. Are you Chester?

LOCKE: (ANGRILY) Oh, that's my birth name.

Locke glares at Katrina as she shrugs back nervously.

LOCKE: I am a High Priest Warlock, and my initiated name is Locke.

ENDRA: Oh, is it?

LOCKE: Yes. (POINTING TO BILL) And *his* is Bill.

Endra hears the door open and close to the greenhouse and looks around. In walk Allison and Chuck.

ENDRA: Oh Allison and Chuck. It's wonderful to see you together. I take it that things are going well?

CHUCK: (LAUGHS) Well? Now you know why we are late.

Chuck leans over and kisses Allison. Allison pretends to be embarrassed.

ALLISON: Oh Chuck.

BILL: Oooh, looks like somebody has bedhead.

LOCKE: Hey, I didn't realize this was going to be a couple's class. (SNICKERS)

KATRINA: Well Locke, you know, we can always make this a couple's class.

THULA: Hey, that's not what Endra is about!

ATHENA: Endra's classes are to be taken seriously. This isn't about couples or sex.

LOCKE: (STANDS UP) Well that's not what these two brought in. (POINTING TO ALLISON AND CHUCK) And I am serious. I am ordained in The Order of the Head Warlocks.

JESSICA: How did you get that title? What did you have to do to get it?

LOCKE: (STILL STANDING, WAVES HIS HAND IN HER DIRECTION) Pfft . . . You don't know who you're talking to.

ENDRA: Take your seat, Chester.

LOCKE: My Wiccan name is Locke. It's my initiated name. And that is what I go by.

ALLISON: Gosh Endra, we're really sorry. We didn't mean to cause a problem.

ENDRA: Problem? No problem my dear. Let's begin class. (LOOKING AT LOCKE) Are you going to stay standing through the whole class?

Locke grumbles and sits down.

ENDRA: Okay. Energy is elusive if you make it, but it doesn't have to be. Let's talk about it a little bit more . . .

Endra's voice fades off as the scene ends.

SCENE 3: END OF CLASS

Class has ended. Attendees are leaving the greenhouse. Allison and Chuck approach Endra first.

ALLISON: That was a great class Endra!

Chuck puts his hand around Allison's waist and pulls her close.

CHUCK: (WHISPERING) Endra, do you ever do anything related to the Kama Sutra?

ENDRA: Oh, you don't need that. Have fun exploring the energy of love together. Also, I do have a book coming out on the energy of love. I'll let you know when it's complete.

CHUCK: (WHISPERING TO ALLISON) Maybe we can write our own Kama Sutra.

ALLISON : (GIGGLES) Oh Chuck.

ENDRA : Sure. Enjoy the energy.

Allison and Chuck leave just as Jessica approaches Endra.

JESSICA: So what is the next thing I do Endra, you know, to move up a level?

ENDRA: There are no levels dear. Just work with the energy.

JESSICA: When can I officially use this energy? You know I haven't finished book three yet.

ENDRA: Well, you can use the energy anytime you like. But, if it makes you feel better, you can finish book number three first.

JESSICA: Okay. Will you be coming in The Dark Cauldron again?

ENDRA: Not so sure my dear. But be well.

Jessica leaves. Thula and Athena approach Endra.

THULA: That was a wonderful class Endra!

ATHENA: Yes it was! When is your next class?

THULA: Yes, we don't want to miss it.

ENDRA: I'm not sure at the moment. But I will definitely keep you updated.

THULA: Yes, anything. If it's a new book, a new class . . .

ATHENA: Because you know, Endra, you are the best.

THULA: Yes. The absolute best. (LEANING IN AND WHISPERING) Despite what that dope says.

ENDRA: Okay girls. See you again soon!

Athena and Thula leave. Bill, Maggie, Allisa and Jane walk by.

BILL AND MAGGIE AND ALLISA: (TOGETHER) Bye.

Bill, Maggie and Allisa walk out.

JANE: Oh, Endra. There is a traditional full moon celebration going on tomorrow night. Are you going to be there? We can save you a seat.

ENDRA: No. I won't be there.

JANE: Well you know Endra, you are very talented. Do you work with a coven?

ENDRA: (LOOKS AND SMILES) No.

JANE: Well, we would love to have you at ours. That is if it's okay with Locke. (LOOKS BACK AT LOCKE)

ENDRA: I don't partake in covens. Goodbye Jane.

JANE: Goodbye.

Jane walks out the door.

KATRINA: Come on Locke, let's go. Let's get a coffee or something. (WALKS BY ENDRA) Bye.

LOCKE: You go ahead. I'll be right behind you.

Katrina leaves.

LOCKE: (POINTS TO TIM, MOTIONING AFTER YOU) You go ahead.

Tim walks up to Endra.

TIM: Thank you. That was a good class. I got a lot out of it.

ENDRA: (LOOKS KINDLY) Thank you. You are a good student, Tim. You are quite gifted.

TIM: You know, I'd really like to keep on top of any other books or classes you have. Keep me in the loop.

ENDRA: Certainly.

TIM: (LEANS IN TO HER) Do you want me to stay behind and help you? (WINKS) Clean up? (NODDING IN LOCKE'S DIRECTION)

ENDRA: No. I like being around the herbs and flowers. (WINKS BACK) They always have my back.

Tim leaves.

ENDRA: (LOOKS UP AT LOCKE) So, still here?

LOCKE: (WALKS UP TO HER DESK) Well, you know, you missed a few points that are very important that you didn't bring up.

ENDRA: Chester, just go home.

LOCKE: What? It's Locke. (SHRUGS) Hey, if you partner with me, I will let you into the coven and teach you what I know.

All of a sudden a stream of pollen passes between them, causing Locke to sneeze uncontrollably.

LOCKE: (SNEEZING) Ahhh-choo! Ahhh-choooo! (HOLDS UP HIS HAND) I'll be seeing you soon. (EXITS SNEEZING)

ENDRA: (TO HERSELF) See me? You can't see yourself.

Endra shakes her head and walks away. She packs up, locks the door and leaves Henry's Flower Shop.

***

ACT 2

THE NEXT DAY, ENDRA'S OFFICE

Endra is in her office on the telephone, speaking to Donald, a previous client.

ENDRA: Oh, Donald. You lost the accent. So, things must be going well with Wendy? Oh, that's wonderful.

Endra hears sounds.

ENDRA: (TO HERSELF) Is that the elevator?

Exiting the elevator on the second floor steps Locke. He is dressed all in black.

LOCKE: (TO HIMSELF) Second floor. Now where is she? Hah! She is no match for me.

Locke passes the first office, Rita's Blow Out Bar.

LOCKE: (LOOKS INSIDE AND SNICKERS) All those dames in there. Having blow jobs? Hah! Funny. I'll come back here afterwards.

Rita, owner and hairdresser at the Blow Out Bar, notices Locke walking by, from inside, and shudders. She quickly peeks out her doorway in Locke's direction as he arrives at the second office.

ENDRA: (STILL ON THE PHONE) Hmm, are you calling me from a hallway Donald? Are you walking? (PAUSES) No. No, Donald. I just hear footsteps loudly. I didn't know if it was coming from you.

Locke stops at the second office door.

LOCKE: (READS) Dionne Sanders, Ph.D., Expert. Expert? That should be plastered all over my door.

Locke reaches Endra's door and stands outside hearing voices inside.

ENDRA: (TO DONALD ON THE PHONE) What was that Donald? Oh, yes, I heard you, but . . . (TO HERSELF) What is going on?

Outside Endra's office Locke has taken a spray bottle from his cape and is spraying around Endra's office doorway and reciting.

LOCKE: I am Locke the High Priest of the Grand Wizards of the Emblem of the Deuces.

To the North (SPRAYS TOWARD THE TOP OF THE DOOR QUICKLY MOVING)

To the East (SPRAYS TO THE RIGHT QUICKLY)

To the West (SPRAYS TO THE LEFT QUICKLY)

To the South (SPRAYS TO THE BOTTOM)

LOCKE: I command you to bow to me. You will succumb to my powers. With this spray of intimidation, I make it so.

ENDRA: (GETS UP, STILL ON THE PHONE) Donald, I have to go. Goodbye.

Endra hangs up and waves her hand with a strong gesture towards the door.

ENDRA: Enough of this!

Outside, Locke gets too close to where he sprayed, slips on the floor and falls on his hip.

LOCKE: Ouch!

Locke reaches up to grab onto the wall for support but gets a hand full of splinters.

LOCKE: What the . . . (LOOKS AT HIS HAND) Geez . . . (CRAWLS TO HIS FEET) I have to get out of here.

Locke limps down the hallway as fast as he can. Rita, working on a client, notices Locke limping by. Locke exits the building and leaves. Endra packs up her stuff and heads home.

***

ACT 3

CAPTAIN COFFEE SHOP

Locke is standing by a table and Katrina races in.

KATRINA: I just got your text Locke. I came as fast as I could. Oh, this Captain Coffee has the best coffee.

LOCKE: Never mind that, did you get me those painkillers?

KATRINA: (HANDING HIM A BOTTLE) Yeah what happened?

LOCKE: Never mind. Are you going to help me or should I call Maggie or Alissa?

KATRINA: No. No. No Locke. I'll do it. I'm here. I can help you.

LOCKE: Take this list down. I need you to get me a dozen eggs, and some honey.

KATRINA: Honey? That's potent. What are you doing?

LOCKE: Just get it. And some wolf's hair. Get that too.

KATRINA: How the hell am I going to get wolf's hair?

LOCKE: Never mind that. If you want to be my High Priestess, you'll figure it out. Watch and learn.

KATRINA: Tell me. Tell me. I want to learn. Are you working on a potion?

LOCKE: It's more than a potion. Now, my powers reign supreme. At all costs. Never forget that.

KATRINA: No. No Locke. I get it. Never question you Locke.

LOCKE: Then get me those things and I want them by 8 o'clock tonight.

KATRINA: I'll do my best Locke.

LOCKE: You'll do it. Or you'll pay.

KATRINA: (WITH FEAR IN HER EYES) I'll do it. I'm just gonna grab a coffee.

LOCKE: Do it now. Or I will make it so you end up with Bill for eternity.

KATRINA: Ewwww. I'm leaving now Locke.

Katrina rushes out. Locke goes up to the counter.

LOCKE: Give me a cup of coffee to go.

BARISTA: How would you like it?

LOCKE: I want it black. Isn't it obvious? And hurry up.

The barista gives Locke the once over and then gives him a dirty look.

BARISTA: (PUTS THE LID ON LOOSELY) Here you go.

Locke grabs the cup, and spills coffee on himself as he growls and leaves the shop.

***

ACT 4

ENDRA'S COTTAGE

Endra and Knight are inside eating dinner engrossed in their own company. They are enjoying themselves.

Outside Locke arrives at her cottage. Locke is all dressed in black with heavy black makeup. He is wearing a cape, limping, and walking with a Wizard stick. He is carrying a dozen eggs, a jar of honey, and a bag full of hair. He walks up to Endra's cottage.

LOCKE: This must be the house.

Locke slinks over to the window and tries to peer in and sees Endra talking and a dark figure beside her.

LOCKE: There she is. What kind of a fool does she have bamboozled in there? Ahh, what do I care?

A tree limb cracks and falls very close to Locke.

LOCKE: Whoah. That was close.

Locke looks up.

LOCKE: Hey, that's not a bad idea. Maybe this tree is telling me I can climb up it and do some damage upstairs.

Locke climbs up the tree and looks over into the window.

LOCKE: Ahh, perfect. No one sees me.

Locke climbs further up the tree and reaches for the window. The honey jar falls out of his hands, breaks and splatters honey all over the bush below.

LOCKE: Damn! (BRUSHING IT OFF) Well, I still have the eggs and wolf hair. (PATTING THE BAG) Damn Katrina. This better be wolf hair.

Locke secures the eggs and hair in his cape and reaches over to the window a second time. Just as he thinks he has the window lever moved, he loses his balance, slips and falls out of the tree and lands on the bush below, and becomes covered in honey.

LOCKE: Ah, at least this bush saved me. And I didn't land on my bad hip. (FURIOUS) Ahh. Geez. I've got honey all over my new cape. You've got to be kidding me!

Locke gets up on his feet again, just as some hair falls out of the bag and gets stuck on his cape.

LOCKE: Oh great.

Locke inspects the hair on the cape.

LOCKE: Okay, I get it. I get it. This honey saved me. It worked like glue to keep the wolf hair on my back. That will protect me.

Locke moves and pulls out the eggs from his cape.

LOCKE: At least I still have these eggs. Takes me back to the days when I was a teenager egging houses. I have a good aim. I had a pretty good arm.

Locke opens the egg carton and picks out two eggs, putting the carton on the ground. Closing his eyes, he holds two eggs up to the moon.

LOCKE: I, the powerful Locke, High Priest of the Emblem of the Deuces command you to do my bidding.

LOCKE: (FOCUSING ON THE EGGS) From the chicken they have hatched for my sole purposes. And with that it is so. So mote it be.

Locke overextends his right shoulder as he winds up and throws both eggs at once in the darkness.

LOCKE: Oh damn! My shoulder! I can't do any of this tonight.

Suddenly Locke hears a buzzing.

LOCKE: What the hell is that?

In the darkness, Locke gets up, rubs his shoulder and hears the buzzing even louder. Locke looks up to the moonlight and sees a swarm of bees heading towards him.

LOCKE: What the . . .? Oh shit! I hit a nest!

Locke picks up the cartoon of eggs and starts to run towards the street.

LOCKE: I'll have to save these.

Running with a limp, holding his shoulder, he keeps heading down the street, dropping his cape.

Inside the cottage Endra and Knight get up and walk towards the front door. Knight opens the door and picks up a bag on the ground.

KNIGHT: What's this?

ENDRA: Is that . . . fur? Has an animal been hurt?

KNIGHT: No. I'm not sure what this is. It's not real. Maybe it's what they call faux fur.

***

ACT 5

ENDRA'S OFFICE, THE NEXT DAY

Rita knocks.

ENDRA: Rita? Come on in. What can I do for you?

RITA: (KIND OF SHELL SHOCKED) Actually I wanted to check on you Endra. Are you okay?

ENDRA: Sure. Why are you concerned about me?

RITA: I am nervous for you Endra. There was a man that came by the office yesterday. He was dressed all in black. I saw him by your office and he scared me. And one of my clients said she saw the same man in the coffee shop and he looked really angry. I'm nervous for you Endra. I wanted to make sure you are okay.

ENDRA: Oh, I'm fine.

Just then the elevator opens.

RITA: Oh, that may be my next client.

Rita pokes her head outside and quickly shuts the door.

RITA: Ohhh! It's him! Should we call the police?

ENDRA: That's who?

Endra opens the door and looks down the hallway.

ENDRA: Just go back to your shop dear. His bullying days are over.

RITA: You're sure?

ENDRA: Yes.

Rita leaves Endra's office and walks down the hallway nervously avoiding any contact with Locke. She hurries past him. Endra steps away from her doorway and walks to her window. Locke storms down the hallway. His face is all red and swollen. He's walking with a limp and his shoulder is dragging, out of alignment with his body. He arrives at Endra's office door.

LOCKE: (POINTING HIS FINGER) I have something to say to you. You are not going to hide behind closed doors anymore with me, Endra. And you're going to listen to me.

Locke steps over the threshold into her office. Endra, still at her window, picks up a book of matches.

LOCKE: Pah! Some matchmaker you are. I'm the High Priest of the Emblem of the Deuces. And you lady, have met your match.

Endra strikes the match and lights an herbal mixture of sage plant and frankincense oil.

ENDRA: I know who I am and of this, I have no doubt. I have all that I could ever need: beauty, support, love and guidance.

LOCKE: Look at me when I am addressing you.

Endra continues by the window, and rubs her hand along the bark of a plant.

ENDRA: There is nothing more beautiful than nature itself. It knows what it is and acts from that. The bark on this plant embraces what it is. It never pretends to be something it is not. Nothing can surpass the beauty of that nakedness.

Endra dips her hand in the dirt of the plant.

ENDRA: Earth supports us all, and provides nourishment from above and below. There is no support more grounded than the earth's.

Endra places some of the plant's dirt around a candle. Endra lights the candle and places it next to the herbal mixture.

ENDRA: And as this dirt first surrounded the wood, it now surrounds this candle. There is no guidance brighter than fire. Fire and guidance and clarity are always mine.

Endra pours water into her chalice on the windowsill.

ENDRA: Water expresses the love that is always at our side. Nothing runs deeper than the depths of the oceans.

Endra opens her window wider.

ENDRA: And wind carries forth this clarity. It clears interactions, leaving the truth nowhere to hide.

LOCKE: Hey! I'm the High Priest here. I demand your attention. I am the powerful Locke, High Priest of the Emblem of the Deuces. I am the most powerful, most significant.

Endra cocks her head towards the wind and whispers, as if repeating.

ENDRA:
>The desire for significance breeds
>its opposite, its pair,
>The result is insignificance, suffocating its mate,
>demanding its fair share.

The candle sparks and crackles. Endra peers into the candle, the flame. She sees a dark figure coming forward.

LOCKE: I am the High Priest . . . Priestess . . . Poostus . . . Wait... what is this?

Locke is temporarily dazed and confused.

ENDRA: (STARING OUT THE WINDOW) I am a significant part of a significant and abundant All. I know who I am. I am created by the nature around me. I am an ultimate being from the ultimate source of which I came. Beauty, support, love and guidance, surround and create me. Of this, I have no doubt.

LOCKE: What is happening? I can't think. I can't remember. What's my name again? Wait a minute? Warlock? War? Is it Wizard? The Wiz? Of the deuce? Shit, why can't I remember who I am?

Locke bursts into tears.

LOCKE: What is happening to me? Endra, have you forced me to lose my power? What are these thoughts I am having?

Endra keeps her focus on the candle in front of her.

LOCKE: (SOBBING) I can't stand these thoughts. I will not go back there. I am not that person anymore. You are a

Sorcerer, Endra. And you cannot force me to go back there. Forget this. I have to get out of here. These thoughts are too painful.

Locke walks towards the door, sobbing harder.

LOCKE: I can't go back there. I can't. I am out of here. I need to find my people. They know who I am. They will help me. The heck with you Endra. You are so mean. I hate you.

ENDRA: Go home Chester.

Locke punches the door as he walks out, and grimaces. He grabs his wrist and cries even harder.

ENDRA:
All I allow in my space is the truth,
being firmly planted in who I am.
Others have forgotten the truth
of who they are, the reason they are here
and how to take care of themselves.
The truth is my sword and my shield.
Living in the truth allows me to be me.

Endra blows out the candle, locks the door and heads home.

***

ACT 6

ENDRA'S COTTAGE

Endra is walking up the path to her cottage. Knight meets her at the door. They embrace, and he gives her a long kiss and holds her extra tight.

KNIGHT: How was your day, mi inamorata?

ENDRA: (SIGHS) Oh, nothing extraordinary.

Knight grabs her hand and they walk into her cottage.

ENDRA: Interactions are very important for all of us to learn and grow and expand with the energy. And knowing when the interaction is over is just as important.

KNIGHT: I enjoy our time together, Endra. I don't know if I tell you that enough.

ENDRA: (SMILES) Oh, I do too Knight. In ways I could never express.

KNIGHT: Endra, we only bring those people whom we choose into our lives. We choose who is invited in our space and who is not.

ENDRA: Yes. We choose how we spend our time and who we spend it with.

They walk out to the patio and there is a table filled with food and four of their closest friends.

ENDRA: How divine! What a marvelous ending to the day.

***

ACT 7

THE BLUE BOOK OF ENERGY

Knight grabs Endra's hand and they walk further out to the patio. Endra sits down at the table and Knight hands her a

glass of mead and offers a toast. Picking up her blue book of
energy he reads.

KNIGHT: As I read from page twenty-five:

"I am a part of the grand scheme, in alignment with and
in synchronization with its power."

***

THE END

Endra:
Anecdotes
of a Modern Day
Witch

by Polonious

Phase 7:
The Elixir of Words

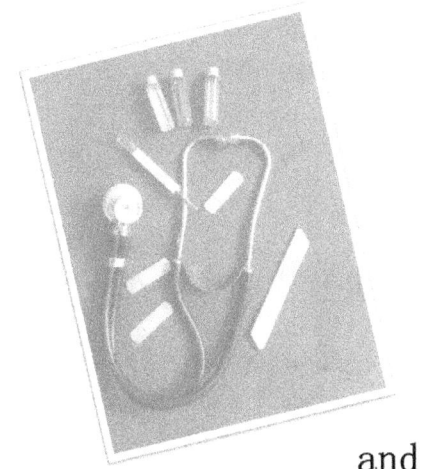

and Digesting the Truth

ENDRA: ANECDOTES OF A MODERN DAY WITCH

Phase 7 – The Elixir of Words and Digesting the Truth

CAST OF CHARACTERS (in order of appearance):

ENDRA.........................*Energy maven living in Windover.*
PAULIE ABRUZZI......*Client of Endra's*
TONY ....*Maintenance/Repairman*
                           in Endra's building
JONATHAN ....*Works in Endra's office building,*
                           an Attorney
RECEPTIONIST ....*Front desk receptionist at*
                           "Center for Herpes"
NURSE ....*Nurse at "Center for Herpes"*
DOCTOR......................*Head doctor at "Center for Herpes"*
KNIGHT ....*Endra's companion and lover*

EXTRAS.......................*Patients in waiting room looking*
                           scared and lost.

SETTINGS IN WINDOVER:

♦*Endra's Office*   ♦*Jonathan's Office*
♦*Park outside Endra's office*   ♦*Inside Jonathan's Car*
♦*In Doctor's Office: Waiting Room & Exam Room*
♦*Endra's Cottage*

Phase 7: The Elixir of Words and Digesting the Truth

ACT 1

ENDRA'S OFFICE

Endra is on the telephone with Paulie. She is nodding her head, close to frustration.

ENDRA: (INTO THE PHONE) Uh-huh. Uh-huh . . .

PAULIE: Yeah, I just talked to my friend Jimmy Hunt, you know the big matchmaker. He's now at DeservingLove.com. Yeah, I guess they ran his own practice out of business. Do you know anything about that Endra?

ENDRA: No.

PAULIE: Yeah, I guess he's doing pretty good now. He got himself a good job and a nice bonus check. Yeah, I should introduce you sometime. Maybe you could go do some work with DeservingLove.com?

ENDRA: (WITH DISGUST) Work for DeservingLove.com?

PAULIE: You know, Endra. I also put my profile on Buddy Bank. It's free and a lot of people look at it, you know. My Buddy Bank has 300 Bills on it.

ENDRA: Bills?

PAULIE: Yeah, it's like a like. I put my picture up with a couple of townies they set me up with.

ENDRA: Oh . . .

PAULIE: Yeah, my last date and I got a lot of those bills. You know, likes.

ENDRA: What does that mean?

PAULIE: Well, it means I should consider going out with her again.

ENDRA: So, you go out on a date and put up a picture of you as a couple and people decide whether you should go out on another date or not?

PAULIE: Yeah. It works really well. And hey, maybe they are looking for more help. You know, you can work with them. Give them my name. They'll give you a piece of the action. I hear there are some pretty big bonuses being distributed there.

ENDRA: Oh.

PAULIE: And the dates and couples that people don't like, oh, that can be pretty rough. One's bald, one's fat. No one wants to be Buddy with anyone like that! But I do pretty good on that. People like me.

ENDRA: Was there something you called me for?

PAULIE: We're buddies now and I thought this might be good for your career, Endra. Besides, you're on my payroll, right E?

ENDRA: E?

PAULIE: Yeah, I call you "E" to all my friends.

There is a knock on the door.

ENDRA: Come in.

Tony, the Maintenance/Repairman in Endra's building comes in. Endra puts up her finger and mouths "One minute" to Tony.

ENDRA: (INTO THE PHONE) Okay Paulie. Time's up. Goodbye.

TONY: Hi Endra. I just wanted to stop in. Something is wrong with the lock on your door. And the door is a little bit off balance. I walked by the other day and there was a breeze coming through on the sides. I think it just needs to be rehung. Is it okay if I do it now?

ENDRA: Oh sure Anthony.

TONY: Hey Endra, do you want to see something funny?

ENDRA: Sure.

TONY: Look at this. Dionne, the expert next door, wrote an expert editorial piece she hopes will be published in "The New York Times." And she went on and on about it. And she asked me to drop it in the mail. And look how she addressed it.

Tony laughs and puts the envelope on Endra's desk. Endra looks at the envelope and reads.

ENDRA: (LAUGHS) The New York Rimes? Did she mean "The New York Times?!" Oh, what a mistake. Well, she's the expert.

TONY: I know. I know. (PAUSES) Hey, Endra, do you have a minute? I wanted to ask you something.

ENDRA: Of course Anthony. I have a spot open.

TONY: What do you think about that new shop coming in across the street? You know, The Mercantile? What's your take on it?

ENDRA: My take?

TONY: Yeah. That's a buddy of mine from the gym who is opening that store. He's a good guy and he asked me if I wanted to invest.

ENDRA: Oh . . .

TONY: Yeah, he needs some money and is offering me equity or I could just give him a loan and get interest. So I'm not sure what I want to do.

ENDRA: It sounds like a math problem to me.

TONY: That's true. It is. And I've made some good money in real estate so the math part I know well.

ENDRA: So, what is it Anthony?

TONY: Well, this buddy already has a small shop doing really, really well. This new shop will be double the size and I think he might be going in a little over his head. So I'm not quite sure what I want to do.

ENDRA: Why do you think he is offering you this opportunity?

TONY: Well, I've known him for a while now. We work out at the gym together. And he asks me for a lot of advice. He knows I've made a lot of money and he values my opinion.

ENDRA: So, what you say to him and whether you invest or not will certainly have an impact on his confidence, as well.

146

TONY: I guess so. I think he is impressed with me and likes the way I look at business. Everyone in the gym comes to me for advice.

ENDRA: So what are you thinking?

TONY: I know real estate, but I don't really know retail. So this would be a big gamble, for me.

ENDRA: So, your advice is just as important to him as your money.

TONY: Yes.

ENDRA: So the words you choose will either break down his confidence or empower him.

TONY: Geez, I never thought of it like that. I guess you're right. Hmm, it certainly is a gamble, either way.

ENDRA: Yes Anthony. But you are a smart man.

TONY: A smart man only gambles with the amount of money he is willing to lose. I don't know how much money I'm willing to lose on this one.

ENDRA: So with your friend and the words you use, wouldn't it be the same kind of investment?

TONY: So it's an investment, whether I use words or money. Oh, I get it.

ENDRA: And that may be the only cost you decide to incur. What you focus on is your choice.

TONY: Hmm, the guys at the gym keep telling him that he is crazy, it's a lot of money, and he will never succeed.

ENDRA: Well, their intent may be different than yours.

TONY: Intent?

ENDRA: Yes. You know he listens to what you say. So your words have power.

TONY: (REPEATS) My words have power. The other guys are negative, so I can either be negative too, or be positive?

ENDRA: Exactly.

TONY: So, I am choosing which one to be? And the choice I make is powerful.

ENDRA: Now that you know that, you can't not know that. Unless you choose to play ignorant.

Endra moves over towards the door Tony has been fixing.

ENDRA: Is everything aligned perfectly, now, Anthony?

TONY: (FINISHES WITH THE DOOR) Got it all fixed. See, that was easy Endra.

ENDRA: Easy indeed.

Tony leaves.

***

ACT 2

ENDRA AND JONATHAN

Endra goes downstairs and enters Jonathan's office.

ENDRA: Oh, Jonathan. I have a funny story. Remember that DeservingLove.com? (LOOKS AT JONATHAN AND STOPS) Hey, what's going on with you?

JONATHAN: I have a lot on my mind. I just got some bad news.

ENDRA: Why don't you take a break? Let's go out for a walk and talk.

JONATHAN: Okay. I can only go for a short one. I have a doctor's appointment in an hour.

Endra and Jonathan leave his office and the building. They head to the park.

ENDRA: So, what's going on?

JONATHAN: It appears I have Herpes of the Gastrointestinal Tract.

ENDRA: What is that? And what does that mean?

JONATHAN: Well, I got a phone call and I guess one percent of the population gets it and if it's not treated it can be fatal.

ENDRA: I've never heard of that. Why don't you start at the beginning?

JONATHAN: Well, I burp after I eat and they say that if you burp after you eat, that's a sign that you have it.

ENDRA: What? Jonathan that makes no sense.

JONATHAN: Endra I'm serious. They may have to take out my intestines and do reconstructive surgery.

ENDRA: Surgery? That's a little extreme.

JONATHAN: Well, I read somewhere that if you burp after eating a meal, or spicy food, it could be a sign of something serious. I went to see the doctor. He smelled my breath and did a urine test. And he believes that it is a classic case of Herpes of the Gastrointestinal Tract. You know they say one percent of men get it and it's a growing epidemic amongst non-gay white men.

ENDRA: (SARCASTICALLY) Yeah, single, tall with dark hair, right?

JONATHAN: Endra, they are telling me I have to get an ultrasound on my intestines.

ENDRA: Jonathan, this might not be as serious as you think. Maybe just a change in your diet and working on your stress is all that's needed. I can imagine that stressing out over this is only going to make these symptoms worse for you.

JONATHAN: I, I just don't know what to do . . .

ENDRA: When are you leaving for the doctor's appointment?

JONATHAN: Now. I should get going.

ENDRA: Shall I come with you?

JONATHAN: Well, if you can I would really appreciate it. Thanks Endra.

***

ACT 3

JONATHAN'S DOCTOR'S OFFICE

Jonathan and Endra are standing in front of a door that says "Center for Herpes." They enter and face the receptionist.

JONATHAN: (TO RECEPTIONIST) Hi. I'm Jonathan DeMarco.

RECEPTIONIST: (IN A LOW VOICE) Yes, we are expecting you.

JONATHAN: Gee. There are a lot of people here.

RECEPTIONIST: Don't worry. We are going to take care of you. We are on your side and we are going to help you fight this. We support all of our patients, honey. And we stand beside them.

ENDRA: He hasn't been formally diagnosed with anything.

RECEPTIONIST: Well, either way, we are on your side. So you have a seat and the doctor will be right with you.

Jonathan and Endra sit in the packed waiting room.

JONATHAN: Look at all these people. They all look like they're dying.

ENDRA: I wonder what they looked like before they got here.

Endra and Jonathan look around the office again. Patients are walking around with big long faces and look afraid and lost.

NURSE: (CALLS OUT) Jonathan.

Jonathan gets up and the nurse motions for him to follow her.

NURSE: I am so sorry about your diagnosis.

ENDRA: (FOLLOWING THEM) He hasn't been diagnosed yet.

The nurse sadly looks back at Endra and taps Jonathan on his shoulder.

NURSE: I'm sorry. But remember, many people have had this and still live long lives.

Endra rolls her eyes at the nurse's comment. The nurse opens a door and the three enter the examination room.

NURSE: First we need to go over some things. Have you been actively digesting?

JONATHAN: (SITTING) Umm, yes.

NURSE: Do you go out to eat with others or alone?

JONATHAN: Yes. I kind . . .

The nurse cuts him off and Jonathan looks at Endra who rolls her eyes again at the nurse.

NURSE: Is there any history of burping in your family?

The nurse reaches for a white gown.

JONATHAN: Well, my great grandmother had indigestion.

NURSE: Oh no.

The nurse changes her mind. She puts the white gown back and reaches for a red gown instead.

NURSE: Here, put this one on. We're going to get you ready for your ultrasound.

ENDRA: So, he just gets an ultrasound? But you didn't check for anything else.

Out in the hallway, singing can be heard. It is someone's birthday and the singing gets louder.

NURSE: (HEARS THE SINGING) Oh, I have to go. The doctor will be in soon.

JONATHAN: But wait, why do I have to wear the red gown?

Nurse exits.

ENDRA: Are you sure that these people have your best interests at heart, Jonathan? You are nothing more than a statistic here.

JONATHAN: But the studies show . . .

ENDRA: Rubbish.

Out in the hallway the singing stops. A minute later the doctor walks in wiping frosting off of his face.

DOCTOR: (LOOKS AT ENDRA) Okay. My patient all set for an ultrasound?

ENDRA: What are you looking at me for? I'm not the one wearing the gown.

DOCTOR: (LAUGHS) You aren't. Are you?

ENDRA: Doctor, no one has checked for anything else but this one diagnosis.

DOCTOR: Oh, so you're not the patient, but now you're the doctor. Hey, I'm the one wearing the white coat. (PATS HIS CHEST) I'm the doctor. I'm the expert.

The doctor walks to the side door holding his hand out for them to follow.

DOCTOR: Okay. Get up. Let's go into this side room. Go ahead and get up on the table.

They all enter the dark room and the doctor shuts the door behind them. The doctor pulls the gown up to Jonathan's chest, puts gel on his stomach, and begins to move the probe of the machine around.

DOCTOR: (LAUGHING HEARTILY) Hey, maybe we can get the game on. It's supposed to be a double header.

ENDRA: This is hardly a game, doctor.

DOCTOR: Don't worry about it Mother.

ENDRA: (LOOKS FURIOUSLY AT THE DOCTOR) Mother? What do you mean Mother?

DOCTOR: Well, you're mothering him. (LEANS TOWARDS JONATHAN) Don't worry. We'll get you through this.

Endra sighs disgustedly.

JONATHAN: When you look at it will you be able to give me a diagnosis, right now, doctor? Or is this something I have to wait to hear about?

The doctor is moving the ultrasound probe around humming, hardly listening to Jonathan's worry.

DOCTOR: (HAPHAZARDLY, JOKINGLY) Sure partner. It's the bottom of the ninth. I can get you a diagnosis in the next minute or two. Ohhh. Oh. Oh.

The doctor stops and squints at the monitor screen. Immediately, Endra leans into Jonathan and whispers.

ENDRA: Jonathan, do you really believe you are sick? It's time you started asking yourself how you feel and stop listening to what everyone else is telling you.

Endra moves her chair and leans in further.

ENDRA: Jonathan, if you need time off, you can have it. You don't need permission or an excuse to have time off. Wouldn't it be nice to take time off and enjoy it?

JONATHAN: (LOOKS DEEPLY INTO HER EYES) Yes.

The doctor is still peering intently at the monitor screen.

DOCTOR: Wait a minute. I think I see something here. We better check this out. (PUSHING DOWN ON JONATHAN'S STOMACH) I see something on the screen.

ENDRA: (LEANING IN) Isn't that something on the screen?

DOCTOR: Yes. Oh, you see it too? This must be serious.

ENDRA: No. On the screen.

JONATHAN: What is it? What is it? Is it . . .?

DOCTOR: It's a spot. On the screen.

ENDRA: Yes. It's a spot. ON THE SCREEN.

Endra moves closer to the screen with a handkerchief in her hand and wipes the screen. The spot disappears.

DOCTOR: Ahh. It must've just been a passing bubble of gas. Well, it looks like you hit a home run today. You have a clean bill of health.

JONATHAN: Are you sure about that doctor?

DOCTOR: Well, it's all clear. Okay partner. Why don't you get yourself dressed? Next time you'll be in a white gown. You're fine. Just lay off the beans.

As the doctor leaves the room, he motions to the nurse.

DOCTOR: Mark this down as another successful case.

The doctor shuts the door.

JONATHAN: Endra, was that really a spot on the screen? (PAUSES) Or did you turn it into a spot on the screen?

ENDRA: (SMILES) Let's get out of here. These people are toxic.

Jonathan and Endra leave. They are driving in his car and Jonathan arrives at her cottage.

JONATHAN: See you in a few weeks, Endra. I think I will take that time-off diagnosis and fill the vacation prescription.

ENDRA: I'm glad you made that decision Jonathan. You're a really smart guy. You should listen to yourself a little bit more often. Enjoy. See you when you get back!

***

ACT 4

ENDRA'S COTTAGE

Endra and Knight are relaxing, in her bedroom. Lying in bed, Knight playfully props his arm up on a pillow. The pillow's tag flops out.

KNIGHT: What is this?

ENDRA: (LAUGHS) Oh, the tag usually goes on the inside when you put the pillow in the pillowcase.

KNIGHT: Why is there even a tag?

Knight holds the tag in his hand and reads.

KNIGHT: Under penalty of law, this tag is not to be removed. (LAUGHS) Were you fearful of removing the tag, Endra?

ENDRA: (LAUGHS) Am I fearful?

KNIGHT: Well, the words command you not to remove it.

ENDRA: The words are only powerful when they are read, my dear. Otherwise, they are just tucked inside, lying at the bottom of the pillowcase, on a tag. Unread and unspoken.

KNIGHT: And when the words are thought of and spoken they have power.

ENDRA: Yes. Otherwise they are unacknowledged.

KNIGHT: And now as they have been expressed, are you fearful of removing the tag?

ENDRA: Now what would I have to be fearful of? They are just words and not mine. And certainly not from one I care about.

KNIGHT: How true, mi inamorata. (LEANS OVER TO KISS HER)

ENDRA: Knight, there are only a few people's words who have that much influence over me.

KNIGHT: Yours?

ENDRA: Yes.

KNIGHT: And?

Knight pulls her closer to him and laughs.

ENDRA: Yours.

Knight leans over and turns the light off.

***

ACT 5

THE BLUE BOOK OF ENERGY

In Endra's bedroom, on the nightstand, Endra's blue book of energy lies open to page ninety-four. The following invocation pulses as candlelight flickers on the words around it:

"I am responsible for the energy behind each communication in which I engage."

***

THE END

Endra:
Anecdotes
of a Modern Day
Witch

by Polonious

Phase 8:
A Different
Transmission

THE PAPERS
OF
STAVALTIX

ENDRA: ANECDOTES OF A MODERN DAY WITCH

Phase 8 – A Different Transmission

<u>CAST OF CHARACTERS (in order of appearance):</u>

ENDRA ....*Energy maven living in Windover.*
GRANT ....*Radio personality at Gossip Free Radio*
CONOR.........*Intern at Gossip Free Radio*
CAROL ....*Caller for Gossip Free Radio*
ELIZABETH ..*Caller for Gossip Free Radio*
ABRAHAM ...*Caller for Gossip Free Radio*
ROLAND ....*Caller for Gossip Free Radio*
HILLARY ......*Caller for Gossip Free Radio*
HENRY ....*Owner of Henry's Flower Shop*
AL ....*Endra's client*
VOICE FROM LINE ....*Person in line at Harkin Fish Market*
MOOSHI ......*Works at Harkin Fish Market*
HARKIN STAFF ....*Woman, at Harkin Fish Market*
HARKIN STAFF ....*Man 1, at Harkin Fish Market*
HARKIN STAFF ....*Man 2, at Harkin Fish Market*
SISTER ROBERTA......*Busybody nun*
CLERK.........*Random worker at Harkin Fish Market*
MAN ....*Random customer at Harkin Fish Market*
LOLA FLYNN..............*Customer at Harkin Fish Market*
KNIGHT ......…...............*Endra's companion and lover*
FIRST, SECOND, THIRD ....*Endra's Visitors*
FOURTH, FIFTH, SIXTH... ....*Endra's Visitors*
EXTRAS ......*People in lines inside and outside of Harkin Fish Market.*

SETTINGS IN WINDOVER:

♦*Gossip Free Radio Station*   ♦ *Harkin Fish Market*
♦*Endra's Cottage*

Phase 8: A Different Transmission

ACT 1

GOSSIP FREE RADIO STATION

Endra is at the Gossip Free Radio Station, sitting in a red room, tapping her fingers.

ENDRA: AAAAAAAAA, EEEEEEEEE, IIIIIIIII, OOOOOOOOO, UUUUUUU. MEMEMEMEMEMEMEMEMEEEEEEEEE.

Suddenly the door opens and Grant walks in.

GRANT: Ahh, stretching your vocal cords, Endra?

ENDRA: Good morning Grant!

GRANT: Are you ready Endra? We have to get to the studio. We have 60 seconds to air.

ENDRA: Yes indeed I am.

GRANT: You are going to do great.

Endra and Grant enter the studio. Conor, the intern, hands Endra headphones which she puts on.

CONOR: 30 seconds (AND POINTS TO THE RED LIGHT OVER THE DOOR)

GRANT: Now Endra, be sure if you have to cough or laugh, don't do it into the microphone. Do it to the side. We'll be live, you know.

ENDRA: (SMILES) Okay.

CONOR: When that light is on, you're on. (POINTS BACK ABOVE THE DOORWAY) Here we go 3, 2, 1 and (POINTS TO GRANT)

GRANT: Hellloo Windover. This is Gossip Free Radio in Windover. It's a beautiful day out there and we are lucky because today we have our local matchmaker here, Madame Endra.

ENDRA: I'm not a matchmaker. (STOPS AND TAPS ON THE MICROPHONE) Hello! Hello!

GRANT: It's okay, Endra, you're on!

ENDRA: I'm not a matchmaker, Grant. To be a matchmaker you need to take some foolish course. I didn't take the course so I'm not a matchmaker. I'm just Endra.

GRANT: What? You need a course to be a matchmaker? I can understand a watchmaker. But a matchmaker?

ENDRA: So it seems.

GRANT: Really? So what's the difference between a matchmaker and what you do?

ENDRA: I deal with energy. I look and see what's in front of me and I work with the energy around me.

GRANT: Continue . . .

ENDRA: If you are trying to define what I do in terms of a matchmaker you would need to ask one of them. I work with energy. And I align two people whose energy connects.

GRANT: So you get people dates by working with energy.

ENDRA: (WITH SARCASM) Oh, I'm sorry. I'm not allowed to use that word.

GRANT: What word?

ENDRA: That word.

GRANT: The word "date?"

ENDRA: (SMILES) That's it.

GRANT: So I'm confused . . .

ENDRA: So, people come to me. I sense their energy and I find out whose other energy is best suited for them, at the moment.

GRANT: Can you explain in a way that our listeners will understand better?

ENDRA: A matchmaker just deals with people. I deal with energy.

GRANT: So, you don't call yourself a matchmaker. But the word in town is that you have the ability to find the most perfect people for those seeking a match. And your success rate is astronomical. Yet, you, Endra, are not a matchmaker?

ENDRA: (SARCASTICALLY) I'm sorry. I am not allowed to use that word and my name in the same sentence. But yes, I am very good at what I do.

GRANT: Whoa, the lines are flashing. We have a wild crowd out there today. We'll be taking your calls in just a few moments as we now pause for a quick commercial break.

GRANT: (MICROPHONE GOES OFF AND GRANT LEANS IN TO ENDRA) This is great. You have a lot of people on the lines.

Grant gets up, stretches, and grabs a small pocket comb from his back pocket and combs his hair. He looks in a small mirror by his microphone, just as Endra catches him mouth the word "perfect" to himself.

CONOR: We're back on in 3, 2, and 1 (POINTS TO GRANT)

GRANT: This is Grant and you're listening to Gossip Free Radio, and we are talking to Endra. The Maaatch . . . oops. (SHUFFLES PAPERS) What should we call you?

ENDRA: Others have termed me an Energy Collaborator.

GRANT: Okay, Energy Collaborator. Before we get started, I just want to point out, you know Endra, I like you. You have good energy. I have a nephew and I'm gonna have him come see you.

Endra smiles.

GRANT: She's smiling folks. Endra, this is radio you know. Okay, Conor stop standing around. What do you think we pay you for?

CONOR: I'm an intern. I don't get paid.

GRANT: Never mind that, who is the first caller for Endra?

CONOR: Umm, we have Carol on the line.

GRANT: Okay, Carol. You're live with Endra.

All of a sudden there is a sound of clanging. Clang, clang, clang. Grant looks over to Conor.

GRANT: Hey, Carol do you have your radio on, or is that wine clinking in the background? We're getting some feedback here.

CAROL: Oh, sorry. Those are my bangle bracelets.

GRANT: Well, just keep them away from your phone because they are very loud. Now, what's your question?

CAROL: Umm, okay. Well. Hi Grant. I always listen to your show. I love your show.

GRANT: Oh, thanks Carol. That's nice to hear. I always love to hear from a fan. But you must have a question for Endra?

CAROL: So, you say you are not a matchmaker, you're an Energy Collaborator. So what are your credentials? I have a big problem and there could be dire consequences and I can't just take any advice. I need solid, expert advice.

GRANT: Can we just get to your question?

CAROL: Well, my girlfriends keep telling me that I am stuck in a relationship that is not good for me. I mean my friends tell me I should just kick him out. They say that I have no life and that I should just start seeing other people. So, I'm kind of trying to figure out what to do . . .

ENDRA: I'm no expert. But it sounds to me like your girlfriends are pretty much solving your problem for you.

CAROL: Well the only problem is that if I let him go I am stuck going to those online dating sites that have crazy people on them. I mean just the other day, my friend told me some guy threatened to cut her head off and put it on a pole.

GRANT: Whoa, put her head on a pole? What whack job did she dredge up? Maybe you should just stay with the guy you are with.

Grant looks at Endra who shakes her head and shrugs.

ENDRA: I have nothing to add to that.

Again, there is a sound of clanging. Clang, clang, clang.

GRANT: Oh, there's that sound again. We better end this call. Thanks Carol. Conor, who's next?

CONOR: On line three we have Elizabeth and her boyfriend Abraham.

GRANT: Okay. Lisa and Abe, you're on.

ELIZABETH: Hi this is ELIZABETHHHHHHHH OOOOOH

ABRAHAM: This is Abraham. Don't mind Elizabeth. Sometimes she goes on and on.

ELIZABETH: NO NO NO NO NO. That isn't true.

ABRAHAM: LALALALALA. Yes it is.

ENDRA: It sounds like you are perfectly matched. What question could you possibly have for me?

ELIZABETH: Well there is good energy and bad energy. What kind of energy do you work with?

ENDRA: I just work with energy.

There is a tapping sound that comes into the station.

GRANT: What's that? Is that tapping? Is someone typing me a fan letter? Conor, what are all these noises? This is radio folks.

CONOR: Why don't you ask Abraham?

ABRAHAM: Oh, sorry about that. I was just tapping on the table here. We are doing a ritual to keep the bad energy out.

ENDRA: Bad energy?

ELIZABETH: It is better to stay in good energy and stay in the light. I let the light shine brightly from me and it leaves my heart center and I project that.

Endra motions to Grant with a big shrug.

ENDRA: By focusing on light energy, or good energy, you are emphasizing or enhancing dark, or evil energy, for yourself. And only yourself. There is just energy.

ELIZABETH: Oh, no, you are wrong Endra. There is good and there is evil energy. I have seen it. I have experienced it. And I know this for a fact. You cannot tell me that it does not exist.

GRANT: Hold your horses Lisa . . .

ELIZABETH: No. No. No. I have seen it. My friends have experienced it. It's a darkness. It's real. It's on our Earth. Mother Earth is trying to conquer it.

GRANT: Lisa, wait a minute. Hey, Lisa . . . can you land this plane?

ELIZABETH: And you know what? I have to stand up to it. If you don't distinguish between good and bad energy you could get yourself into a lot of problems. I have to stand up to the bad energy. And it is my soul's purpose in this life. .

Elizabeth keeps talking and Grant motions to Conor with a line across his neck for him to cut Elizabeth off. Endra nods her head in agreement.

GRANT: Oops. All that tapping caused us to lose that caller. Okay Conor, who's next?

There is a loud, ear piercing squeak.

GRANT: Caller, turn off your radio. Conor aren't you telling these people to turn their radios, appliances, TV's, basically everything off when they talk to us?

CONOR: I don't understand it. I've been interning here for two years. Don't you think I know that by now? I don't know what these noises are.

GRANT: Two years? Aren't intern stints supposed to be for six months?

CONOR: Either they couldn't get anyone to replace me or anyone to work with you.

GRANT: So you mean you've been putting up with me for two years and haven't been getting paid? What's wrong with you boy? (TO ENDRA) He's the best intern we've ever had. We're gonna keep him for another two years. He doesn't know that yet. (TO CALLER) So caller, who do we have on the line?

ROLAND: I'm Roland and I'm a shaman.

There are sounds of squeak, squeak.

GRANT: What the heck is that squeak? Your chair? Can't you use your shaman skills to fix it?

ROLAND: Listen, a shaman is not a fix it guy. A shaman is an earthly healer that can access the ethereal world.

GRANT: What the heck did you just say? Can you translate any of this Endra?

ENDRA: Oh, he's on an island by himself.

More squeaks are heard and Grant looks at Endra and Conor in bewilderment and mouths "What's that noise?" and Conor shrugs his shoulders and mouths "Not on our end."

ROLAND: I've studied for two years at the Shaman Institute. I'm a licensed shaman and am wondering if Endra is licensed as an energy worker or not.

GRANT: Are you really concerned about her credentials or did you want to ask her a question? Because I've known Endra for years and she is an amazing Energy Collaborator. So I am telling you that her credentials are top notch. So either you ask the question or get off our line.

Grant looks at Endra and winks twice. Endra looks and grins.

ROLAND: Well, I wanted to ask her. I am a shaman. I also build websites and I also do some bookkeeping. So I was wondering if she is looking for any kind of interns or if I can help her. I noticed she doesn't have a website. Is there anything I can do? Because I am looking for some work.

Endra holds her hand up towards Grant motioning that she will answer.

ENDRA: Roland, is it? Roland, why don't you send your resume and a nice cover letter to the radio show? And if there is something I can find for you I would be happy to share it. Don't call us. We'll be in touch if something comes up.

GRANT: Next! I'm just pushing the button Conor. I don't want to even know who it is. Hello, you are on the air with Endra, Conor and me, Grant.

HILLARY: AAAAAAHHHHHH, I finally got through! This is Hillary.

Grant's eyes get big and he shrugs, putting his hand over the microphone.

GRANT: (OFF AIR) Can it get much worse than this? (ON AIR) Who is this? Julie Andrews roaming the hills? Are the hills alive out there for you?

HILLARY: OOOOOHHHHHHHHHH. You're so funny Grant. AHHHHHHHHH.

GRANT: Ah, okay. Why don't you tell us what you called for? Who are you again? Hillary? What's your question?

HILLARY: Wellll, I've been having fun listening to this show. It's a great show and I call all the time.

GRANT: I think I would have remembered you.

HILLARY: Well, I too have heard that Endra is amazing and I hope to come by some day and visit with her. But for now I want to give her some good business advice.

GRANT: Okay, go on caller.

HILLARY: Oh, first off, hi ENDRAAAAAAAAAA. Love you, but thought you might benefit if you had a sales pitch. You know, a two minute elevator pitch.

ENDRA: How's this, my dear? Hi, I'm Endra.

HILLARY: Hmmm, interesting Endra. Let me ask you. What is your expertise? What is your currency? AHHHHH. Yes, I did read your books.

ENDRA: Wonderful dear. Good use of the vocabulary.

HILLARY: Yes! I've read all of your energy books, Endra. I love your books and I've heard so many awesome things about your practice.

ENDRA: Thank you dear. So what are you asking me?

HILLARY: I'd like to give you some advice, using your own terminology.

ENDRA: You have the floor.

HILLARY: Endra, you really should define your expertise and your currency. Otherwise, people can't find you and you are just building walls around yourself. But you know, you can get other people to do that work for you. You know. You can negotiate.

ENDRA: Negotiate?

HILLARY: Yeah. Once you define what you really want, you know, via your currency. Then you can negotiate.

ENDRA: Well played my dear.

GRANT: Well I hope someone got that, because you just lost me. I thought this was supposed to be all about dates?

ENDRA: Ah. We are not supposed to use that word, remember, my dear Grant. The show will be what it is supposed to be about. We cannot dictate to the energy. And Hillary, the energy always trumps.

HILLARY: WOOOOOOWWWWWWWWWWW. WHHHHHHEEEEEEE ENDRA

GRANT: You're talking about negotiation. Everyone's talking about credentials and you are telling her that you are supposed to define your expertise. Sounds like we've got experts all over the lines today!

ENDRA: Ah, my dear Grant. An expert is just a glorified historian.

GRANT: (LAUGHS) And historians do love their statues. But don't tell Dionne the resident expert on the second floor.

HILLARY: AHHHHHHHHHHAHHHHHHH

ENDRA: In the book that Hillary is referring to, it explains the difference between your expertise and an occupation. It also shares that your currency is about so much more than money. All are very poignant, especially as they relate to every one of your callers today.

HILLARY: OOOOOOOOOHHHHH. That's SOOOOO COOOOOOOL. My plane is getting ready to board so I have to go. Good to talk to you. I had a great time. Love the show. Love you Endra. Love what you are doing. I love you Grant. You are making radio great again!

GRANT: Well, that's all the time we have for today. Thank you for listening. And be sure to tune in tomorrow, when we'll be interviewing Grandpa from Grandpa's Cider Donuts. Your Mom had 'em. Your Grandma had 'em.

They loved 'em. And you'll love 'em too. And a special thank you to Endra, Energy Collaborator extraordinaire.

CONOR: Great show there, Grant. That's a wrap. We're off the air Endra.

GRANT: You did a great job Endra. You kept your cool. You handled all those calls. I hope you are satisfied with it?

ENDRA: It went exactly as I had expected. The calls were perfect.

Endra starts to gather her belongings.

CONOR: Hey, Grant. Are you heading over to Harkin soon? It's Thursday you know.

GRANT: That's right. Mooshi's there.

ENDRA: Mooshi?

CONOR: Oh, Endra. Every Thursday, Harkin Fish has Mooshi behind the counter.

ENDRA: Mooshi? What kind of a fish is Mooshi?

CONOR: (LAUGHS) Oh it's not the name of a fish.

GRANT: Ooh, I could use a couple of bucks from the lottery.

ENDRA: Is someone going to explain this to me? I'm not psychic you know.

GRANT: Yeah, well, he is.

CONOR: Yeah, yeah, he is psychic.

GRANT: Well, actually, he is sort of a Psychic with Turrets.

ENDRA: A Psychic with Turrets?

GRANT: Is there an echo in here?

CONOR: Yeah, it must go along with all the other sounds we heard today on the lines.

GRANT: Endra, I can't really explain Mooshi. You have to go and see it all for yourself.

ENDRA: Well, you enjoy your fish. I'm heading home.

Endra leaves.

***

ACT 2

HARKIN FISH MARKET

As Endra is walking down the street a male voice calls out to her.

HENRY: Hey, Endra!

AL: Yoo-hoo, Endra! We heard you on the radio today.

HENRY: Yeah, you were great! What were those noises everybody was talking about? Did you hear any noises Al?

AL: I didn't hear any noises.

Henry and Al are standing in line outside of Harkin Fish Market. Endra walks over and stands beside them, noticing it is an extremely long line.

ENDRA: Oh, you both are too kind. Look at this line. (LOOKS UP AND DOWN)

VOICE FROM THE LINE: (TOWARDS ENDRA) Hey! No cutting!

HENRY: (TO THE VOICE) Hey, don't you talk to Endra that way.

AL: Boy. Some people are so rude. (SHOUTS TO THE VOICE) She's not cutting anyway.

HENRY: (TO THE VOICE) You better watch out, Mister. You don't know who you're dealing with.

VOICE FROM THE LINE: Ahhhhh!

AL: I've seen him in Captain Coffee in the morning. He's just a nasty little man.

Henry puts his hand between his shirt buttons and giggles as he motions downward.

HENRY: You know, the Napoleon Complex.

AL: (LAUGHS) Come on. Cut that out.

ENDRA: Oh, you two are darlings.

AL: Endra, the fish here is really good. (SAYS QUIETLY) But we're fishing for something else.

HENRY: Oh, cut the fish puns. If I have to listen to one more of those, I'm out of here.

AL: Endra, we are trying to lure you in here. You have to try some of the fish.

HENRY: Al! Endra, just go in and see what we're talking about.

Endra walks past the line into Harkin Fish. It's a mob scene inside with lines everywhere. Behind the counter is a 4 foot 3 inch woman in 4 inch heels. She is yelling about shrimp. Next to her are two men fighting with a lobster and yelling in another language, while holding the lobster in the air.

A short stocky man with long dark hair is randomly yelling out things as people in the line respond to him.

Endra notices and recognizes the nun, Sister Roberta, from the Lunch Emporium. Sister Roberta is at the counter ordering.

SISTER ROBERTA: Okay. Now I'd like a nice piece of fish. And oh dear, did Sister Nancy want some shrimp and scallops? Yes. She did. What a blessing that I remembered. Okay. Now that will be three shrimp and four scallops. And two pounds of cod. No wait. Four shrimp and three scallops was it? Oh. Yes.

MOOSHI: (YELLS) Babble, babble, babble. Fish out of water. Too much talk. Not good for the soul. God forgive us. Hail Mary pass. A piece of fish.

Endra quickly ducks as a wrapped piece of fish flies over her head.

ENDRA: (SURPRISED) What the . . .?

A man in line catches the piece and hands it to Sister Roberta.

SISTER ROBERTA: Oh yes, my child. That's for me. Bless you.

Sister Roberta turns to the cash register and pays.

CLERK: (YELLS) Oh but we never got you your shrimp and scallops!

Sister Roberta apparently doesn't hear and stops at the lobster tank to bless them.

MAN: Hi. I'd like two pounds of salmon.

MOOSHI: (YELLS) 5, 7, 18, 23. Quick pick 24.

The man quickly writes down the numbers.

MAN: (YELLS) I won 100 bucks last week. (RAISES ARMS UP) Winner!

Others in the line get excited and randomly shout out.

SISTER ROBERTA: (WRITING THE NUMBERS) Blessed Jesus. If I won, just imagine the donations I could make. Of course I could help the dear Sisters, too. And I do need a new TV.

Sister Roberta quickly rushes out of the store.

LOLA FLYNN: Mooshi told me to go to the Emerald Glacier Ranch in Montana. Luckily I went before that big avalanche left that poor woman stranded. The poor woman should have talked to Mooshi before she went. I talked to him and I bumped into someone who gave me a great job back here! Before that, I was out of work for six months. Now thanks to Mooshi, I had a wonderful vacation, met a cute guide there, and now have the money to go back again next year!

Mooshi looks up, turns around and sees Endra. With his sushi knife raised in the air he starts yelling.

MOOSHI: Hello! Hello! Alien! Alien! BOOOOONNNNNNGGGG!

Mooshi then points to another woman in line.

MOOSHI: Baby in oven! Baby in oven!

The woman grabs the hand of the man next to her. They both squeal happily and hug each other.

MOOSHI: Message for Tim! (LOOKS AROUND) Tim. Tim? No fish today.

Endra takes a deep breath, turns around and walks out. In the background Mooshi continues yelling towards her.

MOOSHI: Clang, clang, clang. Airwaves. Transmission received. Over and out.

Endra looks back and smiles at Mooshi and he smiles back.

***

ACT 3

ENDRA'S COTTAGE

Knight is sitting on the front porch and Endra walks up.

KNIGHT: Good evening, darling. You have a package.

ENDRA: Ooh, wonderful, it was clear! I've been working hard all day. Stirring those airwaves.

Knight reaches out and grabs Endra's hand.

KNIGHT: Come. Let's go see.

Endra and Knight go to the back porch and walk out to the vast open sky.

In front of them, a large lighted spacecraft is nestled between some trees. The door opens and six other worldly beings walk out.

FIRST: AAAAAAAAA, EEEEEEEEEE, IIIIIIIIII, OOOOOOOOO, UUUUUUU. MEMEMEMEMEMEMEMEMEEEEEEEEE. Hello! Hello!

The remaining five beings form a semi-circle and begin a beautiful chiming chorus together.

SECOND : Clang, clang, clang. Clang, clang, clang.

THIRD: OOOOOH. NO NO NO NO NO.LALALALALA

FOURTH: Tap, tap, tap. Tap, tap, tap.

FIFTH: Squeak, squeak. Squeak, squeak.

SIXTH: AAAAAAHHHHHH. OOOOOHHHHHHHHHHH. AHHHHHHHHH. AAAAAAAAAA. AHHHHH

ALL BEINGS TOGETHER:
WOOOOOOWWWWWWWWWW.
WHHHHHHEEEEEEE.
AHHHHHHHHHHAHHHHHHH.
OOOOOOOOOHHHHH. SOOOOO COOOOOOOL.

Endra and Knight applaud together.

ENDRA: Bravo! That was beautiful! Oh, you got my messages loud and clear.

FIRST: Very clever of you Endra to reach us that way.

SECOND: We have a delivery for you.

The Third hands Endra a closed box. Endra peeks inside and closes the box.

ENDRA: It's what I asked for. My, how I love the airwaves of online shopping!

FIRST: We have something else for you. We present you with this crystal.

SECOND: You will never find this crystal on this planet.

ENDRA: Oh, it's beautiful.

KNIGHT: (LOOKS AT HER AND SMILES) It is almost as beautiful as you Endra.

Endra hugs each of the other worldly beings.

ENDRA: This crystal is exquisite and powerful. I can do a lot with the sound vibration from it.

FIRST: Those sound vibrations benefit all of us out here too.

ENDRA: The sound emitted from this crystal has the power to make great change.

FIRST: This should also help you to communicate with us instead of using the rudimentary forces you used.

ENDRA: Well, you know me. (SMILES) I use whatever the energy brings. Please come inside and join us.

FIRST AND SECOND: Sure. We have something else to share with you. It's the original manuscript of "The Papers of Stavaltix." One of your kind has tried to recreate it, here. But this one is complete.

ENDRA: Not one of my kind. Hah. Not even close.

KNIGHT: Ahh, "The Papers of Stavaltix." This will be an entertaining evening.

ENDRA: And I can share my blue book of energy with you.

They all enter Endra's cottage.

***

ACT 4

THE BLUE BOOK OF ENERGY

As the wind settles from the spacecraft, the blue book stops turning and opens wide to page thirty-two:

"I do what I love without hesitation."

***

THE END

Endra:
Anecdotes
of a Modern Day
Witch

by Polonious

Phase 9: The Scent of Magick

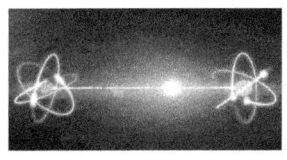

HEISENBERG
UNCERTAINTY
PRINCIPAL

$$\Delta x \Delta p \geq \frac{\hbar}{2}$$

ENTANGLEMENT

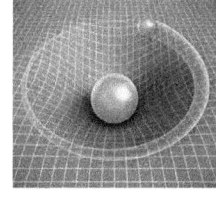

GRAVITY

ENDRA: ANECDOTES OF A MODERN DAY WITCH

Phase 9 – The Scent of Magick

CAST OF CHARACTERS (in order of appearance):

ALYSIA........................*Works in Endra's office building, fashion designer*
ENDRA........................*Energy maven living in Windover.*
JIM..............................*Local Magician*
LITTLE KID.................*Youngster at street fair*
FATHER......................*Father of Little Kid*
WOMAN.......................*Random woman at the street fair*
LITTLE GIRL...............*Little girl at street fair*
ADULT.........................*Random adult at street fair*
PREVIOUS CUSTOMER   *Customer at Jewelry Cart*
CART OWNER.............*Owner of Jewelry Cart at street fair*
FEMALE CUSTOMER 1   *Customer at Jewelry Cart*
JOHN...........................*Husband of Female Customer 1*
FEMALE CUSTOMER 2   *Customer of Jewelry Cart*
MALE...........................*Customer of Jewelry Cart*
FEMALE CUSTOMER 3   *Customer of Jewelry Cart*
AUDREY......................*Owner of Hat Cart*
PHYLLIS......................*1 of 3 elderly friends*
CARMELLA.................*1 of 3 elderly friends*
ANGIE..........................*1 of 3 elderly friends*
BENJAMIN..................*Owner of Fabric Cart*
KNIGHT.......................*Endra's companion and lover*
EXTRAS...........*Samantha the singer, New Threads band, various street fair vendors and attendees.*

SETTINGS IN WINDOVER:
♦*Alysia's Design Studio*   ♦*Endra's Office*
♦*Street outside Endra's office*   ♦*Back of Endra's Cottage*
♦*At the Street Fair: Magician's Stage, Jewelry Cart, Hat Vendor Cart, Old-Fashioned Funnel Cake Cart, Band Stage & Stands, Fabric Cart*

Phase 9: The Scent of Magick

ACT 1

ALYSIA'S DESIGN STUDIO

Alysia is showing Endra her new line of clothing.

ALYSIA: Endra, which one do you think is better? I can only bring a few outfits and I am kind of on the fence with these two. What do you think?

ENDRA: The purple one dear. Always go purple.

ALYSIA: Oh, you mean for the crown chakra?

ENDRA: No. Purple goes with everyone's flesh tones.

ALYSIA: (LAUGHS) That's not what I expected to hear from you. You know, energy wise?

ENDRA: What do you think I'm on all the time? (SMILING) I have a life too, you know.

ALYSIA: Oh, really? I'm not always so sure about that Endra. Now what do you think about this long skirt? I'm trying to bring length back.

ENDRA: Or do like me and just wear whatever you want.

ALYSIA: I like that. Endra style. You're your own fashion statement.

A man with a cape and top hat barges in.

ALYSIA: (POINTING) Are you seeing what I'm seeing Endra?

ENDRA: That depends.

JIM: Excuse me, is this the designer's place?

ALYSIA: (HESITATES) Yeah, I do designs. But this isn't a retail shop.

Jim pulls a bunch of flowers out of his sleeve startling Alysia.

JIM: Please, dear lady, I'm just asking for some simple scarves.

Jim hands Alysia the flowers and she starts to reach for them.

ALYSIA: Oh that's awesome.

ENDRA: (INTERCEPTS HER HAND) Hold on, dear.

Jim ignores their responses and reaches for his other sleeve. He pulls the sleeve out exaggerating, to show that there is nothing inside. The sleeve is empty.

JIM: I forgot my scarves. I need some help. Just a few minutes to curtain call and I need some scarves.

ALYSIA: Well, I don't have any scarves, but I have some fabric I can cut for you.

JIM: Oh, that would be great. If you could just cut four or five colors and make them each two feet long.

ALYSIA: Two feet? Alright, give me a few minutes.

Alysia walks in the back to cut some fabric.

ENDRA: So, may I assume that you are a magician?

JIM: Yes and I am performing during today's street fair, down in the marketplace.

ENDRA: Oh, creating illusions are you? Maybe I'll see you there. (YELLS BACK TO ALYSIA) Are you going to stop by Ben's to get fabric later?

ALYSIA: (FROM THE BACKROOM) Absolutely. Ben's stuff is wonderful. And I usually go there at the end of the night when everyone is gone, to buy up everything he has left.

Jim removes his top hat and taps it against the palm of his other hand. A rock appears.

JIM: Madam, for you, a beautiful crystal rock.

Jim presents the rock to Endra.

ENDRA: Oh what a great trick! Do you need the rock back now?

JIM: No. You keep the rock. Yeah. I guess that was a pretty good trick. Forgive my manners, I never introduced myself. (HE BOWS EXTENDING HIS HAT) I'm Jim Spoon.

ENDRA: Jim, you are quite entertaining. I'm Endra.

Endra puts the rock in her left pocket.

Alysia runs out from the back with multicolored fabric on her arm. She hands Jim the fabric.

ALYSIA: Oh, I love magick! What did I miss?

Jim takes the fabric in his hand and brings his cape around with the other. He opens his arms and the fabric disappears.

JIM: Already in its place. What do you think of that?

Alysia and Endra laugh.

ALYSIA: Oh, that was cool.

JIM: (IN DISBELIEF) Yeah, that was pretty cool. (REACHES FOR HIS WALLET) Please let me pay you for the scarves.

ALYSIA: Oh, please it was extra fabric that I had. Don't worry about it.

JIM: Thank you so much. Please be my guest and come down and see my show. I'm opening the fair.

ALYSIA: I don't think I will be able to get down there but I'm sure you'll be great.

ENDRA: And there will be a lot of illusions to play with down there!

Jim waves and leaves.

ENDRA: Alysia, your designs are striking and they'll pair up just marvelously. But now, I must go back to my office and make a few phone calls.

ALYSIA: What? No clients today?

ENDRA: Hmm, I guess that would depend on how you would define clients, for me.

ALYSIA: Well, by clients I mean people you work with.

ENDRA: There are some energies I work with that never step foot in my office. Then there are those energies that keep coming in my office that I don't do any work with.

ALYSIA: Endra, sometimes you are so complicated.

ENDRA: Well maybe that's because my definition of work is not the same as everybody else's. Ta-Ta.

Endra picks up a piece of fabric and waves it in the air.
Endra leaves Alysia's design studio.

***

ACT 2

ENDRA'S OFFICE

Endra hangs up her phone and goes over to the window which overlooks the street fair.

Outside music plays and Endra puts her head out the window, feeling the sun on her face. Her foot taps along in unison with the band playing. Endra smiles.

ENDRA: Lovely.

Endra hears the popcorn popping from below.

ENDRA: (INHALES DEEPLY) Mmm, that popcorn smells delicious. (STOPS AND LOOKS TO THE SIDE) I think I smell horses? Isn't that funny? Ohh, and the lilacs are finally in bloom. What a feast for my senses!

Endra closes her eyes and feels the sun on her skin.

ENDRA: Maybe now is the best time to head down and get my fabric. And maybe I'll splurge and get myself an old-fashioned funnel cake, as well. Mmm.

Endra leaves her office for the street fair.

***

ACT 3

STREET FAIR

SCENE 1: THE MAGICIAN

Endra arrives at the street fair and sees Jim, the Magician. He is at the first booth and the crowd around him is shouting and arguing.

ENDRA: Wow, it's loud down here. I didn't realize how noisy it was. (SNIFFS AND FROWNS) Oh, is that the popcorn? It smells burnt. (LOOKS AROUND) And where did all those beautiful lilacs go? I can't find them.

LITTLE KID: He's not funny!

Endra sees Jim fumbling on a make-shift stage. Two items fall out of his cape and his magic tricks are unsuccessful. Endra walks closer and looks inquisitively, in disbelief between Jim and a little kid.

JIM: (TO THE LITTLE KID) Well, you're not funny.

LITTLE KID: Daddy!

FATHER: Come on, this magician stinks. Let's go.

Jim walks over to a random woman in the crowd.

JIM: Dear Madam, please for you.

Jim reaches into his sleeve to pull out flowers but instead scarves come out. He hands the scarf to the woman who reaches in and holds it and smiles. She begins to tug.

WOMAN: Oh, this is so funny! How cool!

She continues tugging and pulling, getting frustrated as the line of scarves never ends.

WOMAN: This is ridiculous. It doesn't stop.

The woman loses interest and walks away. The crowd boos.

THE LITTLE GIRL: Daddy, daddy. I like that man's big hat.

Endra instinctively reaches into her left pocket and grasps the rock from the magician's earlier trick. Jim hesitates as a calmness overwhelms him. He takes off his top hat and taps it with his wand. He offers the open hat to the little girl, standing in the crowd.

JIM: Here, for you.

The little girl pulls a rock out from his hat and smiles at Jim.

JIM: For you, my child, a beautiful crystal rock.

The crowd looks on quietly. Endra's attention is drawn to a lilac bush. She leans over to smell it and looks up to her window, while still holding the rock in her left hand.

ENDRA: (TO HERSELF) Now I remember, this is the energy that invited me here.

Endra holds the flower in her right hand and continues to smell it and feels the energy moving in a different direction.

ENDRA: Oh, the spooky action of entanglement, at a distance.

The little girl, who was given the rock from the magician, begins to dance, move and giggle. People around her react to her actions and her smiles. It lightens the mood of the crowd. Endra walks by the little girl and places the rock that was in her pocket on the magician's table. The little girl sees Endra and her rock and walks over to the table and points.

THE LITTLE GIRL: Daddy look! And there's another beautiful crystal just like I have.

ADULT: Hey, that was a good trick!

The crowd cheers and Endra walks past the crowd.

SCENE 2: THE JEWELRY VENDOR

Endra continues further into the street fair.

ENDRA: It is more crowded than it appeared from above. This energy feels heavy.

Endra spontaneously closes her eyes. The sun shines on her face.

ENDRA: (SMILING) Oh, it feels much lighter with the sun. You feel so good on my skin.

Endra reaches her hand up as if to hold the sun's rays and her arm seems to sway towards her right. She opens her eyes and follows her arm and it seems to be resting on a cart of sun catchers. The sun is shining brightly and the sun catchers are sparkling. Endra walks over to the sun catchers on a jewelry cart. Endra picks up one of the sun catchers and holds it in her hand.

ENDRA: Wow. These are much heavier than I expected.

PREVIOUS CUSTOMER: (TO THE CART'S OWNER) Hey, you just ripped me off. I gave you a twenty.

CART OWNER: I gave you your change.

PREVIOUS CUSTOMER: You know what? Keep it. You must need it. Forget it. (WALKS AWAY)

CART OWNER: (LOUDLY) Goddamn guy is trying to rip me off. Trying to get all my stuff for free. I took a day off to be here and I'm getting swindled.

Endra is still holding the sun catcher in her hands, lifting it up and down.

ENDRA: Ahh, the gravity of that statement is quite heavy.

Endra reaches over and grabs a stone.

ENDRA: (TO HERSELF) Yes, this stone is quite heavy, as well.

She places the stone on a piece of felt. The heaviness causes a big indentation in the felt. A few of the lighter stones tumble in towards the heavier stone.

ENDRA: The heavy object with more mass, forces the lighter objects to fall in towards it.

CART OWNER: (ANGRILY) Yeah. All my stones are top quality. That's why they're heavy. Put it here.

The cart owner holds out a black piece of felt that has white star sparkles on it, between his hands. He reaches over and picks up the heavier stone in front of Endra and puts it on top of the felt.

CART OWNER: Look how solid this rock is.

FEMALE CUSTOMER 1 runs up behind Endra.

FEMALE CUSTOMER 1: I want that one! (YELLS TO THE MAN WALKING UP) Come and look at this John. I want this one!

JOHN: (TO THE CART OWNER) Hey, what kind of deals you giving here?

CART OWNER: What do you mean? Everything is a deal here.

FEMALE CUSTOMER 2: (RUNS OVER) Ooh, I love stones.

CART OWNER: Yup, best deal in town! Heaviest stones around!

MALE: (RUNS OVER) Stones? What kind you got?

CART OWNER: Depends on what you want. It's expensive stuff but only the best.

FEMALE CUSTOMER 3: (RUNS OVER) Where's the best one? I want that.

CART OWNER: This one here is one of the very best.

FEMALE CUSTOMER 1: Hey, that's mine! How much?

194

More and more people hover over the cart wanting more stones and demanding only the best.

CART OWNER: Hey, don't worry, I got plenty for everyone! Come and outdo your neighbors!

As this is occurring Endra has already turned around and slowly moved easily through the clear space leaving a fighting crowd behind her.

SCENE 3: THE HAT VENDOR

Endra walks twenty feet and notices some interesting fabric ahead at a hat vendor's cart.

ENDRA: (TO HERSELF) Oh, this is such a different way of using fabric.

AUDREY: (CHEERFULLY) Try it on! Go ahead!

ENDRA: (SMILES) I'm enthralled with the material you used.

AUDREY: Try it on! I think it's so you!

Endra tries the hat on.

AUDREY: See. Oh my God! Hey, we went to high school together. I know you! I remember you! Here, look in the mirror.

Endra, admiring the fabric, looks in the mirror, as the woman runs out from behind the cart and comes up behind her.

AUDREY: Wow, how long has it been? That hat looks perfect on your head!

Endra continues to look in the mirror. Audrey pauses and puts her index finger on her chin. Audrey is mesmerized by her hat on Endra.

AUDREY: You know . . . that reminds me . . . This play . . . I remember the time our class put on this play. You were so good in it, remember? I do. I'm Audrey. Remember me?

ENDRA: I'm sorry dear, you've mistaken me for someone else.

AUDREY: Oh, how can you say that? That's right, you were always such the joker. Didn't you get voted class clown and weren't you on the yearbook staff?

ENDRA: Yearbook staff? To create memories that never existed?

AUDREY: Oh, wait a second. That's right. You always had really colorful clothes. And didn't Josh like you? Weren't you two dating for a while? Did you guys ever get married? As I remember it, my brother was very upset that he wasn't invited to your wedding. My brother never forgot that.

ENDRA: (TO HERSELF) A hat without a head, leaves an open hole to be filled. A big gap. (OUTLOUD) Audrey, your brain is filling your hat's holes with memories that never existed. Just as the brain compensates for its gaps in vision or understanding with what it already knows or is familiar with.

AUDREY: No. That's not true at all.

Endra takes off the hat, picks up another and puts the new one on. She looks directly at Audrey. Audrey backs a few steps away from Endra.

AUDREY: (CONFUSED) Oh, maybe I didn't go to school with you at all. That's funny. Maybe you are right. I don't know you.

Audrey goes back behind her cart. Endra puts the second hat down and starts to walk away.

SCENE 4: THE OLD-FASHIONED FUNNEL CAKE

Endra walks to the old-fashioned funnel cake vendor, hands him some money and he hands her a funnel cake. Endra looks at it, smells it, feels how soft and warm it is, and with a big smile on her face, closes her eyes and takes a bite.

ENDRA: Mmmmm. This is as good as I remember. Yummy.

> *Endra walks further down and sits on the empty stands that were just set up. She listens to the sounds of a new and upcoming local band called "New Threads," who are practicing in front of her. Endra starts tapping her foot along to the beat.*

ENDRA: Mmm, mmm, this is soooo good.

> *Endra enjoys her funnel cake while the band's guest singer, Samantha, steps up and sings.*

ENDRA: Ahh, this is lovely! What a sensational combination: music, singing, food, and the sun. This is wonderful.

> *About twenty minutes later, three elderly women noisily move towards Endra. They are arguing and laughing with each other.*

PHYLLIS: When I get home, those sprinklers better be working.

CARMELLA: Listen, let me tell you something. If those aren't working, you better make sure you call them right away. If you wait it is going to work against you. Let me tell you, I know about these things.

ANGIE: Do we have to walk much farther? Can we sit over here? My corns are hurting me.

CARMELLA: Didn't you get those pads I told you about? Have Harold go out and get them for you.

ANGIE: Ahh, forget about Harold. He has his own problems. I can't get him to do these things for me.

CARMELLA: Sure you can. The walk will be good for him.

PHYLLIS: You know what? Let's go sit over there, on that section of the stands. I have some tissues we can use to wipe off the stands. My pants won't get dirty then.

ANGIE: Why do you always wear those black leather pants? What do you think you're twenty or something?

PHYLLIS: Don't you talk to me about how I dress. Everyone thinks I'm only sixty years old you know.

CARMELLA: Who says that? Men? They only want one thing.

ANGIE: Ewwww. Not my Harold.

Phyllis and Carmella put their hands up and look at each other.

PHYLLIS: What is she talking about?

198

CARMELLA: Did you take your meds today?

ANGIE: I really need to sit.

CARMELLA: (TO ENDRA) Excuse us. Do you mind if we scooch by you?

Endra moves back a little, covering her mouth and breath as the three sit down right beside her. The band has gotten up to take a break. The sun has moved behind the clouds.

ANGIE: Are we gonna be in the sun? I can't be in the sun. My doctor told me it's not good for my skin.

PHYLLIS: I take care of my skin. That's why I look like I'm fifty-five.

CARMELLA: What? Listen Angie. All you need is a little bit of sunscreen. Those doctors can take care of anything.

ENDRA: (LOOKS AT THE FUNNEL CAKE) Hmm. I've had enough. The music, the singing, the food all came together beautifully. But as all things naturally come to an end, so has this lovely lunch.

Endra gets up, climbs off the stands and throws the remaining funnel cake in the trash and walks off. The three women on the stands continue talking.

ANGIE: Geez, we just got up here. I walked all this way and now they stopped playing. And where's the sun?

PHYLLIS: Well maybe the band heard all your complaining and had to take a break.

CARMELLA: Or maybe the cute girl singing got wind of you talking about Harold and she had to go throw up.

ANGIE: That's terrible.

PHYLLIS: (STANDING UP) Gee, I should have gotten up sooner and danced for them. (MOVES HER ARMS AND BUTT AROUND) Then they would have stayed.

ANGIE AND CARMELLA: (LAUGH) Go Phyllis! Go Phyllis! Go Phyllis!

The three laugh.

SCENE 5: THE FABRIC VENDOR

Endra reaches the fabric vendor's cart.

ENDRA: Ahh, there's my Benjamin. That fabric you gave me before was wonderful.

BENJAMIN: Endra! Are you finished with it already?

ENDRA: Yes. I need some more. But Ben, this time, I'm paying you for it. You need to stay in business. You have an amazing product.

BENJAMIN: I could never charge you, Endra. You connected me with my magnificent wife. How in the world could I ever repay you?

Endra picks out her fabric.

ENDRA: You're sweet Benjamin. Thank you. Make sure you give Natalia all my love.

***

ACT 4

ENDRA'S COTTAGE

Endra enters her cottage.

ENDRA: (SNIFFS) Hmm. More of the horses that I sensed earlier today from my office window. A driving force? Passion? Sexual desire? Knight must not be far. Great energy to welcome me.

KNIGHT: (FROM THE BACK OF THE COTTAGE) Out here, mi inamorata!

Endra happily walks to the back of the cottage. Knight is there, blacksmithing. Many wild Clydesdale horses are majestically roaming free. As Endra walks towards Knight, the horses continue to run in all different directions.

ENDRA: Oh Knight! How wonderful! Your horses are here!

Knight laughs as he forges the fire and works with the metal to create shoes for his horses.

KNIGHT: Enjoy yourself Endra and roam free amongst my friends. They are quite the guides.

Endra walks in and around the many Clydesdales. They begin to gather quietly around her.

ENDRA: I guess this is entropy at its best. When I arrived they were running wild. Now look at them, standing here so beautifully around me.

KNIGHT: They are responding to your energy, of course.

ENDRA: We'll see how long that lasts.

KNIGHT: As physics entertained your day, it also entertained your Knight. And now you're Knight can entertain you.

ENDRA: (LAUGHS) Yes. Such wonderful spiritual energy to harness and bathe in.

Knight stops and slowly takes in the vision of Endra enraptured among his horses.

KNIGHT: Ahh, on the subject of bathing. I took the liberty of drawing your bath.

ENDRA: Well, I'm going to take the liberty of sharing it with you.

KNIGHT: Maybe we better go in before the horses pick up on my senses. My work here is done.

Knight quickly puts down his tools. He puts out the fire and light and grabs Endra's hand. They walk into the cottage.

***

ACT 5

THE BLUE BOOK OF ENERGY

The Clydesdale horses behind Endra's cottage roam as the crashing of waves are heard from inside. One horse walks by the blacksmith table. Lying there is Endra's blue book of energy, and it opens to page fifty-two. The following invocation pulses as candlelight flickers on the words around it:

"My journey is filled with plenty of vibrant causes that teach me to act and react, in ways that fill my presence."

***

THE END

Endra:
Anecdotes
of a Modern Day
Witch

by Polonious

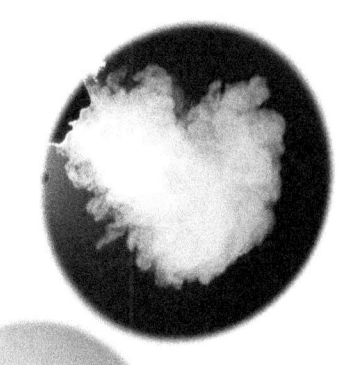

Phase 10: The Mysterious Breath

ENDRA: ANECDOTES OF A MODERN DAY WITCH

Phase 10 – The Mysterious Breath

CAST OF CHARACTERS (in order of appearance):

ENDRA ....*Energy maven living in Windover.*
PEG ....*Endra's client, a mystery writer*
DIONNE ....*Works in Endra's office building,*
                             an Expert
SIGNE...........................*Psychic who hosts a party*
PENELOPE ....*Partygoer, Chiropodist, Alcoholic*
NINA.............................*Partygoer, Arnica Importer/Exporter*
JACLYN ....*Partygoer, Aromatherapist*
LEEANN.......................*Partygoer, Certified Reiki Master*
JASMINE......................*Partygoer, Psychic & Medium*
SANDRA ....*Partygoer, Acupuncturist,*
                             Creator of Blotch Cards
LINDA ....*Partygoer, Entomologist, Researcher*
NILES ....*Husband of Signe*
KNIGHT ....*Endra's companion and lover*

SETTINGS IN WINDOVER:

♦*Endra's Office*   ♦*Endra's Office Building*
♦*Inside Dionne's Car*   ♦*Entrance to Signe's house*
♦*Inside Signe's house*   ♦*Signe's Back Deck*
♦*Signe's Bathroom*   ♦*Endra's Cottage*

Phase 10: The Mysterious Breath

ACT 1

ENDRA'S OFFICE

SCENE 1: PEG

ENDRA: Okay, Peg. Why don't you tell me again what it is you are looking for?

PEG: I've been divorced for five years. I got screwed in my settlement and I decided this time I want to go big. Big guy, big bucks, big appetite for life. And as a writer, I make all of my characters that way.

ENDRA: Oh, so you're a writer?

PEG: Yes. I am a mystery writer although it doesn't always start off that way. I usually just write a story. People love what I write. And in the end, I add in the mystery parts. That works for me.

ENDRA: So, you're a mystery book writer but you don't write it as a mystery.

PEG: No, sometimes I even finish the book and there is no mystery so I have to add it in later. You know, I add in the murder, the murder weapons and the mystery. Is there anything wrong with that?

ENDRA: So, you manipulate your characters, story, and readers. (BREATHES DEEPLY) Instead, why don't you tell me what you like in a man?

PEG: Sure, if we are going to get along, I guess he should come from the same general background as my family. What my family thinks is important to me. But, you know, I'd really like a guy like the ones on the cover of those romance novels. I could stare at them all day. And I do! Seeing them all day makes me hot. Being around those books ain't so bad. (LOOKS AROUND) But you know, I like your office. I could spend an afternoon here. Hey, is that an antique map over there? Where's Gon . . . dwana? There's a character I'm working on that travels and has money and likes men with money who like to dine out. I'm basing the character on me and that character might be the murderer or not. It's a mystery. I haven't decided yet! Eh, I can add that in afterwards.

ENDRA: Okay, so you're a writer. What else can you share with me? (INHALES, EXHALES)

PEG: I manage a bookstore on the coast. And we carry lots of those romance books I like to look at. But, we don't carry porno books. I don't look at those. And the customers that come in . . . well, I base the characters of my books on them. They're my fodder. That's why I have to work there. You know? Working there I get to know all about my customer's lives.

ENDRA: So, you write about people that you know?

PEG: It is my bookstore and they're my stories to tell. I can do whatever I want.

ENDRA: (INHALES AND EXHALES) Okay, time's up. I have the perfect man for you Peg. He has money, he knows everybody, and he likes food. He is the CEO of a local multi-million dollar business. His name is Paulie Abruzzi. (HANDS HER A PIECE OF PAPER) This is his number. You should contact him.

Endra escorts Peg to the door.

PEG: Are you sure?

Peg steps through the doorway.

ENDRA: Yes. Yes. He loves the same treats you do.

Endra begins to shut the door. Peg slightly puts her hand on the door stopping it.

PEG: Oh wait. Have you heard of a company, Ei Alliance?

ENDRA: Yes. They are upstairs. They've published some really good books. A few of mine, as a matter of fact.

PEG: You know, they left ten books at my bookstore, and one of them hasn't sold. I want them to come pick it up.

Endra shakes her head and waves her hand.

ENDRA: Upstairs. Bye. Bye.

Endra shuts the door. Minutes later, Endra grabs her purse and leaves the office.

SCENE 2: OFFICE HALLWAY

Endra steps outside of her office, closes the door and sees Dionne Sanders, Ph.D., Expert, in the hallway.

ENDRA: Good afternoon Dionne. I hope you have a nice night ahead.

DIONNE: Oh, hello Endra. A friend of mine invited me to a party tonight. She is having a group of women over. I'm not sure if I really want to go.

ENDRA: Well, sometimes you're pleasantly surprised over who shows up.

DIONNE: My friend, Signe, is having a group of well-known experts over. She, herself, is considered an expert in the occult. And we experts do have to stick together.

ENDRA: Well, yes, birds of a feather . . .

DIONNE: I suppose they are not so bad. There is just one who sort of doesn't fit in. She's an entomologist. I suppose tonight she is going to bore us about the latest discovery in her field.

ENDRA: What is that?

DIONNE: A few years ago, there were some old beetles found in Antarctica that were related to some ancient land . . . Botswana? Or Godswanta or something like that . . .

ENDRA: (INTERESTED) Do you mean Gondwana?

DIONNE: Yes, that's it!

ENDRA: Dear, would you like some company?

DIONNE: Really? I'd love that. Signe would love to meet you too.

ENDRA: This might turn out to be an interesting night after all.

Dionne and Endra leave the building and walk to Dionne's car parked just outside.

SCENE 3: DIONNE'S CAR

Dionne is driving to Signe's house and Endra accompanies her.

DIONNE: Gee, I was kind of dreading this. I know these women have problems and being a relationship expert they always look to me to fix their problems. But you being here will make things better. It's nice to have a like-minded person with me.

ENDRA: Just take a deep breath. Things may be different than what you expect.

***

ACT 2

SIGNE'S HOUSE

SCENE 1: FRONT PORCH AND INSIDE SIGNE'S HOUSE

Dionne and Endra arrive and park at Signe's house. There are cars all around and they walk up to the house. Signe comes to the door.

SIGNE: Oh, I caught your energy signature. I knew it was you. I knew you were here.

DIONNE: Signe, this is my friend Endra.

SIGNE: Oh, Ennddraa. You have a very interesting energy. Wait, don't tell me, is there a "D" around you? I get a sense of some "D" around you.

ENDRA: Ahh, well Dionne just introduced us and she's standing right next to me.

SIGNE: (VERY SERIOUSLY) No. That's not it.

ENDRA: Well, I don't know. But may we come in?

SIGNE: (WAVES HER HAND) Oh, sure. Come in. But what is it that you do?

ENDRA: Well, you can call me a . . . a matchmaker.

SIGNE: Oh, that's good. That's good. (HOLDING THE DOOR FOR THEM TO COME IN) Because everyone else here is an expert in her own field. You can be the expert matchmaker.

Dionne turns back to Endra and Signe listens.

DIONNE: There are a bunch of needy people here.

SIGNE: (QUICK TO INTERRUPT) That's true Dionne. These people are needy but that's because they are still newbies.

ENDRA: Newbies?

SIGNE: They are not where we are. They are trying to work to get where we are that's why they are needy. (YELLS TO THE OTHERS) Who wants some Chai tea?

PENELOPE: Yah, me! Can you put some vodka in mine? (STUMBLES OVER TO DIONNE AND ENDRA) Hi, I'm the token doctor friend of Signe. I'm a Chiropodist. Can you say that ten times fast?

DIONNE: (TURNS TO ENDRA) Come on. Let's go out on the deck.

SIGNE: (YELLS OVER) Hey Penelope, how long have you been divorced now?

PENELOPE: Ahhh, it's been many moons. (HICCUPS)

Dionne and Endra continue towards the back deck. Someone yells to them.

NINA: Hey! Watch out for that loose plank out there! I scratched my calf over here. Look. Good thing I had arnica. See? I put arnica on it and it's already getting better. Just so you know, I'm the arnica lady. I do importing and exporting of arnica cream throughout the whole Northeast. So what is it you guys do?

DIONNE: I do expert analysis all over.

NINA: Oh, where were you last?

DIONNE: I was in Quebec, Canada.

NINA: Yeah, I've been there. I have sales offices there. (POINTS TO ENDRA) Hey, you. What do you do? Have you been anywhere lately?

ENDRA: (SMIRKING) Yeah, I've been to Timbuktu.

NINA: Oh yeah. I think I've been there too. Yes. I have sales offices there. And I think my old girlfriend and I traveled there once. But we've been broken up for four months now.

DIONNE: Four months, huh?

NINA: Yes. Signe and her husband have been a godsend to me. I don't know what I would have done without them. I came here yesterday because I'm Signe's, you know, closest friend, and I've been cooking since then. I prepared all the food here. Because you know, I'd do anything for Signe.

ENDRA: (TO DIONNE) Which one is the entomologist?

DIONNE: You're Signe's closest friend? I think I am. You're just one of her patients.

Endra leaves Dionne's side and goes outside to the deck.

SCENE 2: OUTSIDE ON THE DECK

Endra enters the back deck. There is food and drink on a table. She pours a glass of water and stands there, as others are talking. Looking from group to group, she is trying to figure out which one is the entomologist.

JACLYN: Oh, yeah, no, I've been divorced and I have a twelve year old son and he keeps having stomach problems. He has to go to school but he doesn't want to. He keeps calling me at work. And it's getting very difficult.

LEANN: Is it a problem at work?

JACLYN: Well, I work for a bunch of lawyers, so yes it is.

LEANN: Oh, maybe Reiki could cure his stomach problem.

JACLYN: Well, I've been working with essential oils because I'm taking an aromatherapy course. But I'm not sure how well they are working.

JASMINE: (COMES OVER QUICKLY) Sorry to interrupt. But I have a message.

Leann closes her eyes and wipes her hands around her body in a circular manner.

LEANN: Not for me, I hope.

JASMINE: Wait. Did you just block me? I got cut off. Did you put up a protection bubble?

LEANN: Yes, sorry. It's just a habit I have.

Jasmine turns around to walk away. She looks at Sandra.

JASMINE: Hey, I'm picking up on something for you. I see changes. Is it job related?

SANDRA: (EXCITED) Good catch! I'm an Acupuncturist but . . .

JASMINE: No. Don't tell me. Don't tell me anything. That's not how it works.

SANDRA: No. No. No. I'm not going to give you anything. Just let me finish. I'm also a . . .

JASMINE: Wait, are you going to say something with money?

SANDRA: Oh my God! I'm also a Banker. I give out loans to new businesses.

JASMINE: A Banker, and an Acupuncturist?

SANDRA: I'm also a Carpenter. I'm in Local 288. A Journeyman in the Carpenters Union. I'm working on my "D" occupation.

JASMINE: "D?"

SANDRA: Yeah. A, B and C are covered. You know, Acupuncturist, Banker, Carpenter. And now I'm working on my "D." (LAUGHS) Let me tell you . . .

SIGNE: (INTERRUPTS, YELLING FROM INSIDE OF THE HOUSE) Hey, did someone say a "D?" I'm still getting a "D." That must be for you Sandra.

Endra drinks a sip of her water and a woman runs past her, going inside the house.

LINDA: Hey, Signe. Do you have my book? I need my book.

SIGNE: Your book? Why do I have to get your book during my party? What do you need that for?

LINDA: Because there's a really big bug . . .

This conversation catches Endra's attention.

NINA: Where? Did you kill it? Did it bite you? I got some arnica here. It's great for bites too.

LINDA: No. I don't want to kill it and it didn't bite me. I want to classify it.

ENDRA: (TO HERSELF) Ahh, the entomologist.

PENELOPE: Classify it? I hope it wasn't in my food. If it was and I ate a bug . . . I'm gonna need a little bit more vodka here, Signe.

NINA: I made the food. There are no bugs in it. You're just looking for a reason to drink.

LINDA: My book, where's my book? Besides, we can look up our ex-husbands in it. I like to classify my friends and ex-husbands by bugs.

Linda runs back outside frantically continuing to search for her book.

LEANN: There's a bug? We should all put up our protection bubbles.

Leann does the same circular hand motion again to create a bubble.

SIGNE: (YELLS) Bug? There aren't any bugs in my house. Maybe it's time for all of us to come on inside. Get out of the heat. Maybe the heat is getting to all of you. Come inside and sit down. We can work out all these issues we have.

As Signe sits on her couch, she motions for her husband to join her.

NILES: Oh, oh, is it okay for me to stay?

SIGNE: Yes, sit right here by me, Puppy.

NILES: Oh, okay.

Niles smiles and puts his hand on Signe's knee and rubs it. The other women go back inside and sit down. Endra and Linda remain outside separated from the others. Endra reaches down beside her and lifts up a book.

ENDRA: Is this the book you are looking for Linda?

LINDA: (GRABS AND OPENS THE BOOK) Oh, yes! Thank goodness! Now, it didn't look like it had wings, but it had a lot of legs. But it didn't have a hard back like a beetle does . . . (STARTS FLIPPING THROUGH THE PAGES)

ENDRA: Beetle! I heard that you had quite the discovery not so long ago.

LINDA: Oh, yes. It was a fantastic, unbelievable discovery! An ancient, rare bug, we named "Ball's Antarctic Tundra Beetle."

ENDRA: Interesting, tell me more.

216

LINDA: Well, the experts are doing their research now, but what we do know is that this beetle is a direct descendant of an ancient line of beetles that once widely inhabited Gondwana. You know, that was a supercontinent that united what we now call Antarctica, Africa, Australia . . .

ENDRA: And South America too, my dear.

Linda looks up from her book, surprised at Endra.

LINDA: Oh, you know!

ENDRA: (INTERESTED) Mmm hmm. And what would this find mean to you?

LINDA: It's so cooool! Just imagine, a 14 to 20 million year old bug, right here, for us to examine!

ENDRA: So, what have they found?

LINDA: Well, the wings weren't intact and we can't tell if it was male or female. It was brown and is apparently isodiametric. And the adult was possibly fully winged although we don't know its gender.

ENDRA: That's nice, my dear. Maybe you can tell me a little bit more about beetles?

LINDA: Of course! I love discussing insects. Let me see. Beetles belong to the order Coleopter. They have two pairs of wings, front and back. The jointed legs of insects are composed of five main segments. These are: coxa, trochanter, femur, tibia, and tarsus. The beetle's head has compound eyes and antennae, of which there are many forms, and some experts call them feelers. Antennae are short, clubbed, comb-like or even hidden in pockets. Hmmm also, in 2015, there was a paper published that confirmed that beetles lived on every continent except

Antarctica. But this discovery changes everything now. Some beetles are water beetles and can hold their breath underwater. Some people consider them natural scuba divers.

ENDRA: Natural scuba divers?

LINDA: Oh let me explain. Most of them have a hard shell, but are able to hold their breath underwater. It's kind of complicated though.

ENDRA: (DISHEARTEDLY) Indeed. Hmm. Maybe we should just join the others back inside.

Linda walks in. Endra stays outside.

ENDRA: (TO HERSELF) Beetles have been alive and breathing underwater before the existence of dinosaurs. These amazing insects create a bubble around them to stay underwater, in some cases, as with water beetles, their entire adult life. This little one, left behind is a time capsule to another world, to our world. This beetle carries with it the life, the air, the breath of a long time ago, and with this discovery exhibits preserved traces of Gondwana's ancient ecosystem, and Gondwana's space. And, who knows what else?

Endra takes a deep breath in and out, then heads inside the house.

SCENE 3: INSIDE SIGNE'S HOUSE

SIGNE: Okay. Who wants to start?

A few of the women start to cry. Endra breathes in and out, deeply.

SIGNE: Let's all have a discussion and see if we can heal each other. Let's just get started and I will moderate. Let's start with . . . How about Jaclyn.

JACLYN: (SIGHS WITH TEARS) My son is troubled. My ex isn't helping. He makes things worse. He's a big dope and I wish he was dead.

The women gasp. Endra continues to breathe in deeply and exhale slowly.

SIGNE: Stop it! We need to give her her space. Go ahead Jaclyn.

Signe smiles at Niles and he rubs her shoulder and nestles his chin in her neck.

LEANN: Well Jaclyn, didn't we talk about it? Aren't you going to try Reiki?

JASMINE: Wait a second, Leann. I'm picking up a grandmother figure.

Leann pushes up her hands to create a protection bubble.

LEANN: Whoop!

Jasmine stops. Signe looks from person to person with a mad face.

SIGNE: Wait a minute. I'm the moderator here. Let's get back on track. Puppy, can you go make some tea for everybody? I think we could all use some tea.

Niles goes to make tea.

NINA: And bring over some of those cannolis I made.

SIGNE: Wait, we are not having dessert right now. The cannolis, the brownies, and the munchkins can wait. Let's just keep going. I am creating a good space for all of this to happen.

NINA: Oh, right. Right Signe. I feel what you are saying. You are really good at that. You are keeping us in line. You know, I'm the one who knows Signe the best here. She helped me during such a bad time with my ex-girlfriend. We are all so fortunate to have the healer right here with us.

Signe sits up straighter in her chair and smiles.

SIGNE: Oh, it's my pleasure to be here with all of you hosting this wonderful soirée with my Puppy Niles.

LINDA: You know what bugs me about my ex. He's like a termite. I can't get him out of my house. And Jaclyn, as I see it, your husband isn't just a dope, he's a gnat. And you know gnats. You have to treat them differently than every other bug. They just don't leave you alone. It's all in my book. And if any of you are really interested, you can go to my website and put in code word "Signe" and get twenty percent off. (PICKS UP HER CELL PHONE) I'm gonna authorize that right now and send all of you the link.

JASMINE: (TO LINDA) You know something. I'm getting a lot of webs around you.

LINDA: Oh, I don't deal with spiders. They scare me.

LEANN: Oh God, spiders! I have to put another bubble up.

JASMINE: It's like you're caught in something.

LINDA: I don't know what you're talking about.

PENELOPE: Yeah, you're like a bug caught in a web. Hey, what's keeping my tea? Maybe just bring more alcohol.

Endra takes in a deep breath and releases a long exhale.

PENELOPE: You know, I don't have these problems. I'm just here for the drinks. I have a new boyfriend. He's into feet, well at least in my bedroom he is. (LAUGHS HEARTILY)

SIGNE: Okay, come on. I'd like to interject at this point that me and Niles have a wonderful relationship that you can all aspire to. (HMPFS CONTENTEDLY) Think of us as role models. Sandra, you've been quiet.

SANDRA: Well, I've been trying to tell you guys about my "D" career. "D" stands for "Dysfunctional Cards."

SIGNE: Oh, you have another business venture. That's the "D" I've been picking up. (TRIUMPHANTLY HMPFS)

SANDRA: I like getting cards they make me feel better. You're all divorced, so let me ask you: If you all got cards while you were going through your divorce, wouldn't it have made you feel better? You know, knowing someone had thought of you during that difficult time?

PENELOPE: Cards to feel better? What are you talking about? I can give you a prescription if you want to feel better.

SANDRA: I brought samples. Here. (HANDS OUT CARDS) Let me know what you think!

PENELOPE: What the hell is this on the front? It looks like a throw up spot. Oh, maybe I shouldn't have said that . . .

JACLYN: Oh, it looks like an ink spot.

SANDRA: Close. It's a blotch of paint that came alive. I call it "Blotch" and I've even trademarked it.

JACLYN: Oh, it's just black and white. Wouldn't it be nicer if it had a scent or some color?

SANDRA: It's what's on the inside that counts. Open it and read it.

NINA: Oh, let me read mine first. I want to read mine first. "Getting Divorced?" and inside "Now every day is Independence Day." (PAUSES) I don't get it. Signe, do you get it?

SIGNE: Of course I get it. That's really funny. Sandra you've done a great job with the work we've done together.

NINA: Oh, now I get it. (LAUGHS UNCOMFORTABLY)

JASMINE: (READS) "Getting Divorced?" and inside "Nobody saw that one coming." (LAUGHS HYSTERICALLY) I would have seen it coming. This one's perfect for me! Of course I would have seen it coming. I see everything coming. I love this one.

PENELOPE: (READS) "Divorced" and inside "Is the ink dry? How about a date?" (LAUGHS)

DIONNE: Hey, what about me? Don't I get one?

Nina hands a card to Dionne.

DIONNE: (READS) "Divorced" and inside "Congratulations! Enough said." (LAUGHS) I deal with relationships and love. That's a riot!

LEANN: Oh my gosh. These have great energy. You should make these for other occasions, Sandra.

SANDRA: I'm so glad you like them. My favorite is "Divorced?" and inside "Meet you at the bank!" You know, because of my other career! (LAUGHS) I've made them for other occasions too.

Endra takes a deep breath unaware of the conversation in the room.

SIGNE: Those cards are great and they would be very helpful with all the self-worth issues that are bleeding into relationships. And I think Dionne would agree with me on this. She is an expert, and my good friend. She gives expert witness statements on relationship issues and is always asked for input by the major TV and radio stations. Isn't that right Dionne?

DIONNE: Thanks Signe. That is a great explanation of what I do. I am the leading expert.

NINA: Oh, what are you an expert of? I don't think you ever told me that?

DIONNE: I have multiple degrees and I am a relationship expert. I work with CNN, MSNBC, ABC News, and all the major news networks. The average person would have a hard time consistently being in front of the camera and being asked all these questions. But I've met a lot of people and they've needed my knowledge.

All the women gasp "ooohh" and "ahh."

SIGNE: Well, that's my friend. What about you Endra? You told me you're a matchmaker.

All the women turn to face Endra with excitement and anticipation.

NINA: Hmm, a matchmaker? Can you find me a girlfriend?

JASMINE: Oh, I see you're going to be in a relationship soon.

NINA: (INTERESTED) Oh, you see me with someone?

JASMINE: I can see you as a caretaker.

NINA: Oh my gosh. That's me. That's me!

NILES: (FROM THE KITCHEN) Yeah! You took really good care of me and Signe when we visited!

NINA: (TO JASMINE) But you see me with someone soon?

JASMINE: I see you around a woman and water. You're arm-in-arm.

NINA: Ohh, maybe a cruise?

JASMINE: I don't know.

NINA: That's awesome.

SIGNE: (FRUSTRATED) Wait a minute. Wait a minute. I have to reel you back in. Ladies, you keep going off topic. We are trying to heal here. (TO ENDRA) So, you said you're a matchmaker.

Endra walks in the middle of the group.

ENDRA: Listen. Why don't we all take a deep breath in . . . and then exhale.

Everyone breathes in and exhales deeply. Niles comes in with tea.

ENDRA: Okay. Why doesn't everyone grab a cup of tea from Niles? (TO NILES) Please bring in those donuts.

NILES: But, we're supposed to wait. That was our dessert. Is that okay Signe?

SIGNE: (MOTIONS FRUSTRATED WITH HAND) That's fine. Nobody's following my directions anyway.

Niles places the munchkins on the table.

ENDRA: Okay. Everyone grab one of the donuts.

The women reach in and grab a donut.

ENDRA: Once again, everyone take a deep breath in. (PAUSES) And breathe out. (PAUSES) Everyone pick up your tea and slowly take a sip. Are you enjoying it? Now, you should each have a bite of the donut.

The women follow her directions.

ENDRA: Now everyone close your eyes and listen to my words. This deep breath will invigorate the stomach and mouth to produce saliva. The tea will prepare the body, and the sugar from the donut will work on the pituitary gland which will, in turn, adjust each of your moods. You each will immediately have a rush of adrenaline and feel much better.

The women follow her directions and begin to sigh independently of each other.

ENDRA: Now, open your eyes and enjoy how much better you feel.

LEANN: Oh, that was amazing.

JACLYN: Yes, I feel so much better.

LINDA: Me too. That was great.

SIGNE: (QUIETLY UPSET) I have to go to the bathroom.

Signe gets up and leaves.

SANDRA: You're much more than a matchmaker. You could be a matchmaker and a healer, you know.

From a distance they hear yelling.

SIGNE: (DISTANTLY) Help! My arm! I need some help!

PENELOPE: Is that Signe?

Nina gets up and runs from room to room frantically looking for Signe.

NINA: Where is she? Don't worry Signe! I'm coming!

NILES: I'm coming too! She was going to the bathroom.

Niles and Nina run to the back where the bathroom is. Nina arrives first and opens the door to see Signe crouched under the sink. Signe's arm appears to be jammed under the sink.

PENELOPE: (FROM THE LIVING ROOM) What's going on?

NINA: It's Signe. In the bathroom. Don't worry. I will take care of this!

Penelope doesn't move and takes another sip of her drink.

PENELOPE: No problem.

NINA: (YELLING OUT) I'm helping her. Niles, grab me the arnica cream in the medicine cabinet. It's on the second shelf on the right side. It's in a green jar marked "A."

Leann and Jaclyn gather in the hallway with Niles, as Nina and Signe are in the bathroom.

LEANN: (WHISPERS TO JACLYN) How does she know where everything is around here?

Jaclyn shrugs.

JACLYN: No one can get in there Nina, to get anything.

From outside, Niles reaches over Nina into the medicine cabinet and grabs a jar. He holds the jar out to Nina.

NILES: Is this it?

Nina, crouched with Signe on the floor, looks up at Niles.

NINA: No. Hand me the green one!

Niles returns the first jar and grabs the green jar and hands it to Nina. Nina starts putting the salve on Signe.

SIGNE: (LOOKS AROUND ANGRILY BUT NOT IN PAIN) Where is everybody?

NINA: I'm working on your arm. I almost have it out. Don't worry.

SIGNE: (STARTS GASPING) Puppy, are you there?

NINA: Okay. You're okay. We have your arm free.

Niles reaches down, picks Signe up and carries her to the couch where she swoons. Nina, Jaclyn and Leann follow.

LINDA: Well what happened? You were in the bathroom and your arm got caught? And stuck? Under the sink?

SIGNE: (SUDDENLY DAZED) I don't know. I don't know. I fell. I don't know what happened.

NINA: Here. I've got some more arnica cream. Let me rub your shoulder, your arm.

LEANN: (RUNS OVER TO SIGNE) How about some Reiki? I can do Reiki on you.

Signe has her eyes closed then slowly opens one eye.

SIGNE: Okay. That will be good.

JACLYN: Do you want me to use some of my oils?

NINA: No. The arnica is just fine for this.

SIGNE: (FAINTLY) Oh, who does the acupuncture here?

SANDRA: Well I do, but I don't have any of my needles.

DIONNE: (TO ENDRA) Do you think we should help?

ENDRA: No. This is orchestrated. There is nothing to do.

DIONNE: (STOPS, AND LOOKS AT ENDRA) Well, I'm ready to leave then. Are you ready Endra?

ENDRA: Yes. I've already left.

Dionne and Endra go over to Signe, who is now surrounded by all her party attendees.

DIONNE: I'm so sorry for what happened Signe. But we are going to have to leave.

228

SIGNE: (OPENS HER EYES SLOWLY) You're not going to stay and help me? I guess there is nothing you two can do for me anyway.

JACLYN: Oh that's okay Signe, we're here.

Signe closes her eyes again and sighs. Endra and Dionne separate from the group and walk to the door.

NINA: I need to get more arnica cream.

Nina walks in the direction of Endra and Dionne, looking satisfied with herself.

NINA: I knew I was going to be the one to help her, to take care of her.

ENDRA: Indeed. You are the caretaker.

Endra and Dionne head outside, get in Dionne's car and drive away.

***

ACT 3

IN THE CAR OUTSIDE OF ENDRA'S COTTAGE

DIONNE: I'm glad you came with me, Endra. I hope it wasn't as bad as it seemed. If nothing else, I enjoyed the ride back and forth with you.

ENDRA: You certainly have some interesting friends.

DIONNE: You know, Endra. I didn't get a chance to ask you about the donut and the tea and the breath.

ENDRA: Yes?

DIONNE: You know, you really did help them. How come you never told me about that before? It's like you kept a big secret.

ENDRA: Secret? Every day people sit down and have tea, and have something to eat with it. I didn't do anything.

DIONNE: Well, with the breath thing . . .

ENDRA: Well, we all breathe. Sometimes we just forget that we are breathing and how powerful that is.

DIONNE: Ohhh.

ENDRA: A lot happens in the breath that people aren't aware of.

Dionne takes out some paper and points to a pen.

DIONNE: Endra, can you hand me that pen? Thanks. And could you repeat that again? I can use that line in my next newsletter and blog post.

ENDRA: Goodnight Dionne.

Endra leaves Dionne's car and goes inside her cottage.

***

ACT 4

INSIDE ENDRA'S COTTAGE

Endra walks in and Knight is pouring a cup of tea.

KNIGHT: A cup of tea, mi inamorata?

ENDRA: (LAUGHS) I think I've had my fill of tea for tonight.

KNIGHT: Hmm, then wine perhaps?

ENDRA: (LAUGHS) Oh, I've heard enough whining too.

KNIGHT: Whining?

ENDRA: Oh, it matters not. I wasn't really there.

KNIGHT: Already in Gondwana?

ENDRA: Yes, and the beetle is here now. Do you know what might have happened to this one?

KNIGHT: Yes. That's precisely why we are going to Gondwana, my love. As a master of surface tension this beetle moves through both worlds. And this one has a lot to tell us.

ENDRA: So, I suppose it's time?

KNIGHT: It sure is. Are you ready to go?

ENDRA: I cannot wait. And I am a good packer, just like the beetle.

KNIGHT: (NIBBLES HER EAR) Maybe I can keep a little bit more of you back here, just for a short while longer?

ENDRA: Certainly my dear. I can focus on where I am, here with you. Later we can focus on where we are going.

KNIGHT: Mi inamorata our journey begins now.

ENDRA: My love, whether I am here or there, I am always with you.

Knight moves closer to Endra as they embrace.

***

ACT 5

THE BLUE BOOK OF ENERGY

Endra and Knight lay on the bed and on the night stand is Endra's blue book of energy. Endra nudges Knight, and he picks it up. They take a deep breath together, and he opens it to page one hundred thirty-five. The invocation pulses and the words flicker, as he reads:

KNIGHT: "I breathe with clarity and presence allowing the All to consume me."

***

THE END

Coming Soon!

The Knight Scripts

Endra: Anecdotes of a Modern Day Witch Joins Knight in His Realm

Phase 11: Knight in his Shining Armour

by *Polonious*

For more information visit:
https://fanlink.tv/EiAlliance

or

contact:
EnergeticInvocations@gmail.com

From the Authors:

If you have any interest in things other than people's stories, complaints and drama, and feel that there is something else out there, you're right, there is. And that's where we are.

Social media, television, movies, other self-help books are unfulfilling. They just perpetuate an empty feeling. If you are interested in what everyone else is doing, keep supporting them. Yet, if you are interested in accessing something else within yourself and all around you, our books help to open the door to magick, science, creativity, and psychic ability.

We work with energy. What does that mean?

Everyone wants to talk to us or be in our conversations. So, we wrote about what we know and have experienced. If you want to be in our conversations, listen to our podcasts. Otherwise, read our books, that's where the energy is.

Find our books on our Amazon Author pages and via the list at the front of this book here: https://fanlink.tv/EiAlliance

Find our archived podcast shows everywhere:

"So What! Now What?"
"Write, Now! with Julie B"
"Your Presence Is Required"
"Let's Talk About Energy, Ours & Yours"
"The Kybalion: A Conversation"
"Ancient Texts – The Genealogy of Energy"
"Oprah! Can You Hear Me? Oprah vs. Donald 2020 and Beyond!"

Find out about our BLOTCH© cards and ebooks, and how Blotch© creates the voice, to say, and hear, that it's okay to be different and not fit in. Blotch© supports others, to be just who they are through his fun, ironic and witty viewpoint.

Follow "Ei Alliance" on:
Facebook, Twitter, Instagram, *Spotify, Medium*, and *YouTube*

EnergeticInvocations@gmail.com

***

www.ingramcontent.com/pod-product-compliance
Lightning Source LLC
Chambersburg PA
CBHW050341030726
47503CB00008B/2559